Wintergreen

Mari Biella

CHAPTER ONE

I STOOD BEHIND the police cordon, watching as the last members of the forensic team tramped out of the woods and into the gravel area of the car park. Dusk fell early at this time of year, and the last of the day's light was beginning to drain out of the sky. They'd done all they could do for one day: the dead man had been moved to the mortuary, and the surrounding area had been scoured for evidence. Before long, the woods would return to their usual peaceful state, as if this brutal disturbance had never occurred. The camera crew from a local TV news programme had left half-an-hour before, and even the villagers, many of whom had been milling around in the car park earlier, had for the most part dispersed and gone back to their homes. I could hardly blame them. It was getting darker and colder by the minute – and not just in a literal sense.

A death – any death – always casts a long shadow, especially in a small community. It would not be a happy Christmas in Wintergreen this year.

One of the few people who were still there paced around slowly, gradually moving closer, until he came to rest a few feet away from me. I had the feeling that he wanted to talk to me, though I couldn't imagine why.

"Aren't you getting cold?" he ventured at length, in a friendly tone.

"I'm okay," I said, wishing that – if this was anything more than an opportunity to exchange some friendly chatter – he would get on with it. The man, however, just continued to stand at my side, looking out over the woods, peering up into the sky.

"There'll be snow soon," he remarked at length. "Cold front coming in from Russia, according to this morning's weather forecast. We might get a White Christmas after all."

"I doubt that will be much consolation to the dead man's family," I replied, glancing at him. As soon as the words were out of my mouth, however, I realised that I'd spoken sharply, more sharply than I'd intended. It was the legacy of living in London, perhaps, where the approaches of strangers were suspect, and almost always discouraged. The man raised an eyebrow, and the corner of his mouth perked up in a strange lopsided smile.

I'd seen him hanging around in the car park earlier, studying the crowd and – I'd noticed – keeping a particular eye on me. It hadn't taken long for me to work out that he was probably a policeman. He wasn't in uniform, of course, but I'd spent enough time around the police to develop a kind of sixth sense about them. I'm an investigative journalist by trade, and I've found that journalists and police officers have one thing in common: they're both very good at watching, waiting, and listening. When you consider the uneasy, distrustful, mutually exploitative relationship between the two professions, it's really not surprising that we've acquired an almost supernatural ability to recognise one another.

Still, I reminded myself, it might not be a bad idea to keep the local police on side, if I could. Sometimes, they were a useful source of information. I leaned towards the man very slightly, and tried to sound conciliatory as I said:

"Sorry. I didn't mean to sound rude. That's what comes of living in London for so long."

"No need to apologise," the man said, shrugging. "I suppose I was a bit tactless. You lose a certain amount of sensitivity, in this job. You have to. Survival instinct, you know."

"You *are* a policeman, then," I said, and he laughed.

"Is it really so obvious?"

"Probably only to me; but I'm a journalist." I turned and looked at him. "Do you know who the dead man is?"

"I'm fairly confident that I know, yes. But there's been no formal identification as yet, and I'm certainly not going to bandy names around in a car park, least of all with a journalist." He looked at me a little more closely. "Do you mind my asking who you are? I haven't seen you around here before."

"I'm just here for Christmas. I'm staying with my mother and stepfather in the village."

"Oh, I see. That'll be the Wallers, I suppose."

"You know them?"

He smiled again. "In a village the size of Wintergreen? Everyone knows everyone."

"I suppose they do, yes."

"Is this the first time you've been here?"

"Yes. My mother and stepfather used to live over in Alverston." Alverston was the sprawling new town, ten miles away, where I'd spent much of my childhood. "They moved out here to enjoy their retirement in peace. Not that they're going to get much peace this Christmas. I arrived a couple of days ago, and my brother's coming down with his wife and kids tomorrow."

"They'll be kept busy, then." He looked back in the direction of the woods, and his smile faded. "They might be grateful for the distraction. All of this is going to cast a long shadow over the village in the coming days and weeks. People can't believe it's happened. You don't expect it, in a little place like this."

I could imagine that this was so. In the short time I'd been in Wintergreen, I'd already found out that it was the kind of place where people left their doors unlocked and the local shop gave credit without asking any questions or demanding any kind of security. It was a big difference to what I'd got used to in London, certainly. But a sudden, mysterious death – a death that might be suspicious – causes you to rethink your assumptions. Perhaps Wintergreen wasn't quite the idyllic, untroubled place I'd imagined it to be.

I gazed at the woods, where the shadows were deepening by the minute. Foxhay Brake, this area was called. It was a popular spot with runners, dog-walkers, and nature lovers. Not the kind of place where you expected a man to be found dead, lying face down in a stream at the bottom of a steep gully. Yet that, apparently, was what had happened. A group of local kids had stumbled upon the body that morning, and had called the emergency services. The first indication I'd had that something was amiss was when several police cars blazed past on the quiet country road, lights flashing and sirens blaring.

"I suppose," I said, turning back to the man, "that a case like this presents quite a challenge to the local force. I don't expect you're used to dealing with such things."

The man returned my gaze, rather coolly now. "You needn't think we're all Keystone Cops in this part of the world," he said. "The investigation will be conducted exactly as any inquiry into a suspicious death, in any part of the country, would be."

"You *do* think it's suspicious, then."

"When a relatively young and healthy person is suddenly found dead we have to consider all the possibilities, which is exactly what we intend to do." He gave me a quick, sharp glance. "For someone who's supposed to be on holiday, you seem to be very interested in all of this."

I gazed at the man for a moment. He was about my age, maybe a few years older. Tall and well-built, he had close-cut dark hair, a rather angular face, and clear blue eyes. The shadows under his eyes, and the slightly strained look in his face, suggested to me that he was either perennially tense or a fellow insomniac, shadowed by exhaustion yet unable to sleep. What struck me most forcibly, though, was the keen intelligence in his eyes. He hadn't been talking with me just to pass the time, that much was clear.

"I can't help but take an interest," I admitted. "I suppose my job has taken over my life, in a way. I'm never really off duty."

"And I suppose you think you've found a story in this."

"No. All I want to do while I'm here is relax." It sounded like a lie, even to me. It had certainly been my intention to enjoy a quiet Christmas in Wintergreen, but my work had a habit of bleeding over into every aspect of my life. Besides, I was a freelancer, lacked even basic job security, and frequently found that I had to work twice as hard as many of my colleagues just to stay afloat. The truth was that part of me was *always* looking for a good story.

The man held my gaze for a moment or two longer, and then, suddenly, held out his hand.

"Detective Inspector Jake Fernsby," he said. His hand was large and rather rough, his grasp firm. "I suppose I might as well introduce myself, since we'll probably be seeing quite a lot of each other while you're here. I'm stationed over in Alverston, but I live here in Wintergreen. I'm a local boy, through and through."

"Catrin Armistead."

"Well, Miss Armistead, if you do decide to write something up, I hope you'll at least try to make it accurate."

"I always strive for accuracy. But really," I added, "I'm not planning to do anything over Christmas except eat, drink, and relax."

We were silent for a moment. Dusk was creeping in fast now, and the shadows were thick and deep in the nearby woods. I wondered what had happened there the night before, and shivered. Even in a small place like this, the darkness was never far away. I'd always known that, of course, but I didn't really want to be reminded of it. Not now.

"You'd better be getting back, before it gets dark," the inspector said. "Do you need a lift?"

I would have preferred a lift to walking back in the near-dark, but my early conditioning kicked in. You didn't accept rides in cars from strange men, even if they were policemen, and even if they might be a source of valuable information.

"Thanks," I said, "but I'll walk."

"Be careful, then. This is a pretty safe little place in general, but you can't be too careful."

I nodded as I turned and began to walk out of the car park. The woods on either side of the road rustled and stirred, and the wind bent boughs and sighed through the undergrowth. Skeletal leaves skittered along the path. I thought of the dead man who'd been found out here, and what could have happened to him, and why. Suddenly I longed to be back inside, surrounded by light and warmth, in a place where the dangers that lie in wait for us can be ignored – for a little while, at least.

I glanced back over my shoulder. A few straggling policemen were still standing around in the car park, and the police cordon fluttered in the wind. Jake Fernsby, standing quietly to one side, was watching me as I walked. I turned my head again, and picked up my pace.

LUCKILY, I DIDN'T have very far to walk. The place where I was staying this Christmas was just a short distance from Foxhay Brake, on the grounds of a local farm. Though I was here to spend the holidays with my relatives, there wasn't enough room in my mother's house for both me and my brother's family, and I'd been given a choice between a sleeping bag on the living room floor and finding some rented accommodation. There hadn't really been any competition. I was past the age when sleeping on the floor could ever be considered fun.

I'd been lucky to find Stable Cottage, I supposed. It had been renovated just a few months before, and the owner hadn't yet found a permanent tenant, so I'd managed to get it cheaply for the duration of the holidays. It was a tiny place, part of a converted stable block on a working farm. During the short time I'd been there, I'd learned what life in the country could be like. A cockerel's cry woke me every morning just before dawn, and sheep sometimes wandered into the small back garden to munch on the grass. In a place like this, London seemed very distant indeed.

It was dark by the time I began to walk up the rough lane that led to Willowgate Farm. A car approached from the opposite direction as I trailed uphill, and the bright glare of the headlights left me momentarily dazzled. The car slowed down to a crawl and then stopped, and my new landlady – Mrs McQuoid, or Lita as she preferred to be known – wound down the window and smiled out at me. She was a small, slender woman who looked much younger than her fifty-odd years, and was a good deal sleeker than you'd expect of a woman who'd lived on a farm for decades. Her blond hair was cut into a sharp bob, and she was rarely seen without make-up and expensive clothes. It was hard to believe that, after her husband's death, she had not only taken over the day-to-day running of the farm, but had turned it into a thriving business.

"Hello, Cat," she said, sounding as cheerful as ever. I assumed that she hadn't yet heard about the dead man in Foxhay Brake, and I decided not to tell her. "Have you been to see your mother?"

"I've just been out for a walk. Learning more about the area."

"There's not much *to* learn about a place like Wintergreen. Is it going to feature in one of your reports?"

I laughed. "I won't be writing any reports while I'm here. I'm just looking forward to relaxing for a change."

"That's just as well. There's not much else to do out here." She shivered. "Lord, it's freezing. Better get in out of the cold. See you later."

She wound up the window again, and the car purred as it turned the corner. I walked the remaining distance to Stable Cottage, which bordered on the farmyard. The main farmhouse, standing at a right angle to it, was dark and silent at this hour, and looked rather sad. Lita lived there alone, or so I understood; her husband was dead, and her only daughter was away at university. I sometimes sensed a core of loneliness beneath Lita's brisk facade, but it never showed. Perhaps she was just too busy to indulge it.

Inside, Stable Cottage had the unfinished, rather cold look of all untenanted properties. There were a few old pieces of furniture, provided by Lita, and some nondescript pictures hanging on the walls, but the place had not yet been stamped with anyone's personality. Part of the former stable – the reason, obviously, for its rather uninspired name – it was a small rectangular space, single-storey, with a rough stone floor and whitewashed walls. It contained little more than a living room with a small kitchen off to one side, a bathroom and a bedroom, all of which suited my needs perfectly.

I set about preparing a simple dinner of the sort I often ate in London: bread, salad, and some soup. I'd inherited my Italian mother's love of good food, but not her culinary skills, and my work left me with little time or energy for domesticity. That, perhaps, was one of the reasons why my marriage had fallen apart. Derek had pretended to be a modern man, but ultimately he'd wanted a traditional home life, with a wife who'd take care of the housework and raise children. He'd never have got that with me. Perhaps he'd have more luck with his current girlfriend, a gentle little art teacher who dreamed of staying at home and cultivating her love for pottery. They'd been together for almost a year, and I wished them well. Despite the pain and messiness of our divorce, Derek and I had managed to remain on good terms, much to my relief.

As I ate, I thought again about the man found in Foxhay Brake. Such information as I'd gleaned so far was both stark and ambiguous, admitting of several possible explanations. He'd been found at the foot of a gully, lying face down in the water. Nobody was sure yet whether he'd died as a result of a fall or drowning, or even whether the cause of death had been something else altogether. Until that was ascertained, every option had to be considered. One such option – suicide – struck me as being highly unlikely. If a man wanted to kill himself, I thought, he probably wouldn't wander out into the woods on a cold December evening and throw himself into a gully so small that he couldn't even be sure of dying as a result. Murder also seemed improbable, and for much the same reason; it would hardly be a reliable way of killing someone. In all probability, then, it was just a sad accident. Perhaps he'd been taking a shortcut home through the woods; perhaps he'd had a few drinks, and was a little the worse for wear. A stumble, a quick fall, a head injury – such things happen rather more often than we like to think. Incidents without reason and without blame. Random mishaps which suggest that, whatever we like to think to the contrary, we live in a rather arbitrary and meaningless world.

A tragic waste of life and a sad story, but – in the larger scheme of things – not a significant one. Not one that I'd be likely to spend my Christmas holidays writing about, anyway. It would probably merit a little coverage in the local media, but it wasn't big or serious enough to go any further. Such was the callous nature of my industry.

Still, something about the case continued to nag at me. When I'd finished eating, I opened my laptop and dragged up a map of the Wintergreen area. The village stood on the western side of a shallow river valley, surrounded by low hills and pastures. On the other side of the river, a quiet B road wound past Willowgate Farm and Foxhay Brake. Beyond that, there were a few straggling houses, generally large and expensive, set a little way back from the road. Someone who lived in one of those houses, or who was returning to the village from there, might decide to take a shortcut through Foxhay Brake, which would be quicker and more direct. Even after dark, it might seem like a reasonable thing to do.

I went to the back door and, opening it, looked outside. The sky had cleared slightly, and a full moon sailed high above the Earth. Foxhay Brake, rolling out beyond the back of the small garden, looked like a rippling silver pool beneath its light. It was beautiful, but – one way or another – it was also deadly.

I was standing and staring out into the night when I felt my heart clench beneath my ribs. I had sensed something moving in the shadows, just beyond the fence that marked the boundary of the garden. I peered into the darkness. I could see nothing, but I felt certain that something was there.

A moment or two passed; and then there was another movement. I saw it clearly this time and, though I couldn't see what it was, I was sure that it was real. A fox, perhaps – but no, it was larger than that. I waited and watched, painfully aware of my own harsh breathing and the skittish beating of my heart.

But there was nothing else – nothing but the sound of the wind and the distant hoot of an owl. Gradually, I felt my stretched nerves begin to unwind. The countryside was full of living creatures, after all, and if I was startled by them it was only because I wasn't used to them. My heart rate slowed, and at length I turned and went back inside.

I kept my doors locked that night, though, just the same. Even in a quiet place like Wintergreen, anything might happen.

CHAPTER TWO

I WAS PASSING the newsagent's shop in the village when I saw the headline on the front page of the local paper, in big, bold print:

DEAD MAN FOUND IN WINTERGREEN NAMED: HUGO MONTBRAY, LOCAL BUSINESSMAN

Montbray's name meant nothing to me. I went into the shop, bought a copy of the paper, and stood outside for a minute or two while I scanned the article. It featured a photograph of the dead man staring at the camera with a complacent, slightly arrogant expression. He had been rather young, no more than forty years old, and slightly flabby, with fair hair. Behind him, a golf course glowed beneath bright sunshine: a fleeting moment of his life, caught and preserved for eternity.

For those who weren't familiar with the village, there was a simple map showing Foxhay Brake's position in relation to Wintergreen. Examining it, I saw that Montbray's house – also marked on the map, along with a photo – had been a large Georgian house just off the B road that ran eastward from the village and passed Willowgate Farm. I remembered driving past the house on a few occasions, and wondering who could afford to live in such a place. The location where Montbray's body had been found, along the footpath that led from the village to his house, lent weight to my suspicion that his death had been a simple accident. Assuming that he had either been travelling to or from Wintergreen on foot that night, taking the path through Foxhay Brake would have cut at least ten minutes off his journey.

Then I read the accompanying article. According to an unnamed police source, Montbray did not habitually visit the village in the evening or drink in the pub there. He had few close friends in the local area, and wasn't a particularly sociable person. When he visited Wintergreen he usually drove, despite the relatively short distance, and he hardly ever went into the woods. He never drank to excess, and was not given to reckless behaviour. His life, it was suggested, had revolved around his work. He'd built up a rather impressive business portfolio for a man of his age; he had owned and managed an estate agency in Alverston, and had invested heavily in real estate. He'd pursued these interests with single-minded dedication, and had as a consequence very little time for traipsing around the woods at night or drinking in the local pubs.

An autopsy had been scheduled, the article concluded, and the results were expected to shed light on the circumstances surrounding

Montbray's death. The police had informed the family, and were continuing their investigation.

Things didn't end there, however. According to a small subsidiary article on the next page, the Montbrays were quite a family. Descending from a long line of local squires, they had dominated the Wintergreen area for centuries, and had apparently acquired a rather unsavoury reputation in the process. Ruthless landlords, harsh employers and inveterate womanisers, they had bullied, lied and ensnared their way to the position they now enjoyed – and, in a twist of the kind beloved of sensationalist reporters, they even had a family curse. According to local legend, a Montbray had seduced a local servant girl in the seventeenth century and had then abandoned her. The girl had hanged herself, but not before placing a curse on the family – a curse that condemned the male Montbrays to violent, premature deaths. This was the kind of folklore that crept up repeatedly throughout the country, of course, and that rarely had much basis in historical fact. If the

Montbrays saw this report, I thought, they could be forgiven for being irritated by it.

I shivered in the chill wind, folded the paper in half, and continued my interrupted walk. My mother and stepfather were expecting me for lunch, and I didn't want to be late. Besides, my brother and his family had arrived earlier that morning, and I was looking forward to seeing them again. Adam was three years younger than me and, when we were growing up together in Alverston and our mother was out at work, I'd often been responsible for looking after him. I'd resented him at the time, but now that we were both adults we got on well. I was proud of him; he'd emerged from our troubled childhood with a degree in biology and a girlfriend, Sandy, whom he'd since married. Both now worked as teachers, and had two young sons, Freddy and Sam. They'd embraced a normal life in a small town, and there were times when I envied them. They seemed happy, anyway, and their marriage was solid, and that was far more than I'd ever achieved.

My mother's house, just outside Wintergreen's heart, radiated seasonal good cheer. A Christmas tree twinkled in the front window, and the few decorations she'd put up complemented the house rather than swamping it. Even now, when the village was stunned by the news of Montbray's death, the place exuded simple contentment and goodwill. As I approached I saw that Adam's car was outside, loaded with bags and suitcases and all the things that a family of four might need to get them through a long Christmas break.

I had just opened the gate when the front door flew open and the younger boy, Sam, ran outside with an indignant howl. Freddy careered after him, waving a water pistol. He pressed the trigger, and a jet of water shot out, soaking Sam's jumper. Sam, apparently seeing any adult as a potential protector, ducked behind my legs and cowered there. Freddy, catching sight of me, stopped and stared. I hadn't seen either of my nephews for six months or so – a long time, for a child – and he probably wasn't even sure who I was.

"Hello," I said, smiling. "Don't you know me?"

"Are you Auntie Cat? Mummy said you were coming."

I nodded, and then said the thing that almost all adults say in such situations: "Gosh, haven't you both grown!"

Sam, still hiding behind my legs, clung to the hem of my coat and let out a mournful little wail. I reached down and scooped him up into my arms, and caught a glimpse of a screwed-up face, convulsed with one of the many small pains of childhood. Sometimes I wondered how Adam and Sandy, or anyone else for that matter, handled being parents. I didn't think I could have endured it.

"Come on," I said. "It's almost Christmas. You ought to be enjoying yourselves, not being mean. Are your mum and dad inside?"

I set off towards the open front door with Sam in my arms, while a sullen Freddy followed close behind, his water pistol dangling from his hand. I'd just set foot inside when a harassed-looking Sandy came out into the hallway, casually dressed and with a glass of mulled wine in her hand.

"Have you been teasing your brother again?" she asked Freddy sharply, and he responded with a surly silence. I put Sam down at her feet, and he wrapped his arms around her leg. She reached down to ruffle his hair, and gave a weary smile.

"Oh Lord," she said, "I can't tell you how much I need this holiday. How are you, Cat?"

"Fine." I gave her a quick little hug, and saw Freddy trailing away disconsolately out of the corner of my eye. The scent of cooking and the sound of soft classical music drifted out of the open kitchen door, and made me think of home. This had always been my mother's dream – a quiet life in the countryside, filled with simple pleasures – and I was glad that she'd finally achieved it. She'd certainly worked hard enough for it. She'd arrived in Britain from her parents' village in Northern Italy at the age of twenty-two, and in the years that followed she must sometimes have wondered why she'd bothered. Her life hadn't been easy: our father had been lost when Adam and I were young, and there was never much money, and she'd had to work like a slave just to keep us all clothed and fed and with a roof over our heads. I don't remember her ever complaining, though she must have felt like it sometimes. Only time, and her eventual, happy marriage to my stepfather, had reversed the tide of misfortune that must once have seemed inescapable.

I had just let go of Sandy when Adam appeared in the kitchen doorway and grinned at me. "Hi, sis," he said, and swept me up into a hug. Behind his back, I saw Mum smiling and my stepfather, Peter, raising his glass in a little salute.

I was always surprised by my family's ability to make me feel relaxed. As a teenager, my greatest desire had been to get away from them and live my own life; now, I sometimes found that all I wanted to do was to go back to them. I supposed they represented something durable, something that I could cling to in this mad, changing world. Perhaps I'd never really appreciated them in the past. I'd been so busy working and worrying and chasing rainbows that I'd forgotten how much pleasure could be found in the simple things of life.

And besides, I just loved them; and that's the most important thing of all.

LATER, AFTER WE'D eaten our lunch of spaghetti, fish and roasted vegetables, and my nephews had trooped off to watch a garish cartoon on TV, the conversation inevitably turned to Hugo Montbray.

"Such a blasted shock," my stepfather said, pouring the last of the wine. "I mean, I never met the chap, but I felt like I knew him through his reputation. Anyway, any kind of death shakes up a village of this size, even if the dead person was hardly likely to win any prizes for popularity."

"Was he disliked around here?" I asked.

"You could say that," my mother replied in an accent that years in Britain had done little to dilute. "The Montbrays had a bad reputation in any case."

"An unpleasant lot, by all accounts," my stepfather agreed. "They really were pretty nasty a few centuries back: horsewhipping peasants, chasing the local virgins, that sort of thing. The worst kind of country squire. They've lost a lot of money and influence since then, of course, but Hugo carried on the family tradition anyway. Fond of money and women, by all accounts, and not too scrupulous about how he came by either of them. There was some suspicion that he wasn't entirely honest in his business dealings, and he certainly broke a few hearts. Some people could be forgiven for not being entirely sorry that he's dead."

"Was it an accident, do you think?" Sandy asked. She looked nervous: she'd come here for a quiet Christmas break, not to contend with rampaging murderers.

"It's the most likely explanation, if you ask me," I said. "The gully where he was found is really very shallow – just less than ten feet deep, according to today's paper. He was unlucky: a fall like that wouldn't usually be fatal. It wouldn't be a reliable way of killing either yourself or someone else, anyway, so you can probably rule out suicide or murder. Obviously, the police have to look into every possibility." I drank the last of my wine, relishing the mellow warmth it brought. "Does he have many living relatives?"

"A few," my mother said. "Not so many these days. His father died some years ago, I think. Diana Montbray – that's Hugo's mother – sometimes shows her face in the village. She volunteers at the church, arranges flowers, helps out at local fetes, that kind of thing. She's a quiet little woman, not at all like her sons. I've spoken to her a few times, and I quite liked her."

"There's a younger brother, too," my stepfather said. "Charles, I think his name is. Never got on too well with his brother: some dispute over an inheritance, I think. Works in a bank in Alverston, or so I understand. Never moved out of the family home, though, despite all the disagreements. I can't imagine what the atmosphere was like there, with all of them crammed in together."

"It must have been hellish," Adam said, shaking his head.

"According to the local paper, the family is cursed," I said, not altogether seriously.

"Oh, that old tale," my stepfather, ever the rationalist, scoffed. "Every family that has been around for a while seems to pick up a few curses along the way. It's the same old story: seduced girl, cruelly abandoned, laying a curse on her tormentors before finishing herself off."

"It all adds to the myth, anyway," my mother said, and gave me a rather sharp glance. "You seem to be very interested in all of this, Cat."

"I can't get out of my work mentality. I'm always on the lookout for a story." I shrugged. "I don't think I'm going to get one in this case, though."

"Jake Fernsby tells me that you were hanging around Foxhay Brake yesterday afternoon."

"Oh, the policeman," I said nonchalantly, and she laughed.

"He referred to you as 'the reporter', you know. I'm afraid he doesn't have a very high opinion of your profession."

"Well, I'm used to that," I said, which was true. Along with bank managers and politicians, journalists tend to be an unpopular lot on the whole. According to a common preconception, we're a bunch of meddlesome, amoral sensationalists who make a living out of hounding people and would sell their mothers for a story. Unfair, of course; but, as with many stereotypes, there is a grain of truth in it. Anyone who wants to get anywhere in such a competitive profession has to be both persistent and inquisitive, and the nature of the modern media makes a degree of sensation almost inevitable. And, if I was being honest, I had hounded people on occasion. I had doorstepped them, questioned them, and pressed them for interviews, quotes and sound bites. I had finagled and exaggerated. I had failed to be entirely honest with people, and had deliberately misled them once or twice. Despite working at the more serious end of the journalistic spectrum, I'd sometimes made an almighty nuisance of myself, and hadn't always won a lot of friends.

My mother was gazing at me across the table, and she suddenly looked rather serious, and almost sad.

"I hope you're not going to get involved in all of this, Cat," she said. "You're supposed to be on holiday, and certain things are better left to the professionals. That's what Jake Fernsby said to me this morning, and I have to say that I agree with him."

"Do you often exchange gossip with him?" I asked, feeling slightly annoyed.

"It's a little hard not to, when he lives in the village and I see him every few days. He's a big part of local life, and he's well-respected."

"You can't help but respect someone like that," my stepfather said, nodding. "He's dedicated to his job and devoted to the village. Besides, he's had to deal with a great many bad things in his life."

"What kinds of things?" I asked, intrigued.

"The deaths of his wife and child, for a start. I think that's quite a burden for anyone to bear."

There was a long moment of silence. I glanced around the table. Adam and Sandy sat quietly side by side, their expressions unreadable. My mother kept her eyes down, as if she couldn't bear to meet anyone's gaze. Lively theme music floated out of the living room, where the boys had begun to watch another cartoon. I felt awkward, and momentarily lost for words.

"What happened?" I asked at last.

"An accident," my stepfather said, shaking his head. "His wife was driving home from her parents' house one day, along the motorway, and their daughter was in the car with her. The weather conditions were bad, I understand, with heavy fog and quite a lot of spray on the roads. Another car came in fast from the feeder lane, and the driver didn't see her until it was too late."

"Oh my God," Sandy whispered, looking pale.

"Horrible," my mother said. "It happened five years ago, but he's never really got over it. He's reluctant to talk about it, though, and he certainly doesn't want anyone's pity. Don't mention it if you meet him again, Cat."

"Of course I won't. What do you think I am?"

"Sometimes I think you don't see people as people. You've become used to seeing them as characters in a story, or sources of information."

I was silent for a moment. Her words seemed unfair, and yet – the niggling little whisper inside my head wouldn't be silent – weren't they also true, at least to an extent? When I tried to analyse my own character, I didn't always like what I found.

"I'm off duty, Mum," I said at last. "I'm not planning to write anything while I'm here, and I certainly shan't be writing about Hugo Montbray."

"I should bloody hope not," my stepfather said, in an effort to lighten the mood. "We'll have enough on our hands these holidays without you careering around interviewing witnesses or pestering police officers. Let's just try to have a nice peaceful Christmas, shall we?"

A COMBINATION OF wine and a heavy meal had left everyone tired and sleepy, and after helping with the washing-up I left, hoping that a brisk walk back to Willowgate Farm would wake me up. I cut through the heart of the village, past the local shop and the ruins of a small Norman castle, and then paused outside the churchyard. I hadn't been inside the church since I arrived in Wintergreen. I'm not an especially religious person, but I've always liked the hushed, otherworldly air of churches, the feeling you have when you step inside that you've left the rest of the world behind. I made my way up the churchyard path, past old and more recent graves, and tried the heavy oak door. It opened with a pained creak, and I stepped into a dim space that smelled of flowers and incense.

Thinking that I was alone, I walked slowly down the side aisle. I took a small postcard from the table, and put some coins into a collection box. The church was older than I had thought, I realised, holding tombs and effigies from centuries before; probably quite a few Montbrays were buried there. Another one would be joining them before too long, it seemed.

I had walked perhaps halfway along the nave when I heard a small sound from up ahead, a sound that I couldn't quite place. I paused and listened. A few seconds passed in silence, and then the sound came again. I peered around the pillar that shielded the altar from my view, and saw that someone was there after all, standing with her back to me.

She was a small lady, slender, and elderly if her stooped posture and white hair were anything to go by. She wore a brown skirt and a drab grey cardigan, dull colours that seemed to fade into the background, and I wondered if this was deliberate: far from seeking anyone's attention, she seemed determined to remain invisible. Looking a little more closely,

I saw what had caused the noise I had heard: she was trimming the stems of some flowers and arranging them in a vase. She was intent on her task, so much so that she seemed to be unaware of my presence.

I walked towards the altar, and my footsteps echoed around the nave. She turned and looked at me, and I saw that her face was drawn and tired, and her eyes luminous with tears. She tried to smile at me, but her smile looked terrible, desolate.

"Are you all right?" I asked, knowing how stupid a question it was. *Obviously* she was not all right, but she was hardly likely to want to discuss her problems with a complete stranger.

"Oh yes, yes," she said, waving her hand. A tear spilled out of her eye and rolled down her cheek. "It's just – just a personal problem. I'll be fine."

"Can I do anything to help?"

"No." She turned and looked at the altar. "Only *He* can help; but His ways are subtle, and sometimes defeat our understanding. We must try to understand, though, mustn't we? We must try to be patient and have faith."

"I suppose so."

She turned back to me, wiping her eyes. "I haven't seen you in the village before," she said.

"No. I'm just visiting. I'm staying here over Christmas."

"Christmas!" she repeated, and gave a frantic little laugh. Then her face straightened again, and she put the last of the flowers into a vase. "Wintergreen is not the place to come to celebrate. It's not a happy place, and never has been — at least not for us. Especially not now. If I were you, I'd leave as soon as I could. This is the last place anyone could possibly want to spend their holidays."

With that, she gathered up the severed stems and scurried down the nave. Her footsteps echoed around the church, and then faded as she pulled open the door and went outside. I stood looking after her, and remembered what my mother had told me about Diana Montbray. *She volunteers at the church, arranges flowers. A quiet little woman.* Was she Hugo Montbray's mother?

I stood still in the empty church, thinking. The short December day was reaching its end, and the light that filtered through the stained glass windows was heavy and dull. The place didn't seem holy anymore, just lonely and sad. I turned and walked down the aisle, towards the door.

Outside, the daylight was draining out of the sky. A crow squawked angrily from a bare branch above my head. I walked quickly towards the gate, suddenly anxious to reach the sanctuary of Stable Cottage. As I walked, however, my eye fell upon two relatively recent graves that stood beneath the spreading branches of a yew tree. Fresh flowers had been placed before the headstones, which were of matching black marble. I stopped to read the inscriptions.

In loving memory of Patricia Fernsby, I read. I looked at the other stone with a sick feeling spreading up from my stomach, and read: *Heidi Jane Fernsby.* I glanced at the dates beneath the name, and saw that Jake

Fernsby's daughter had been four years old when she died. I stood looking at the graves for a while, thinking about the brutal facts they revealed. Then I turned and hurried away from the churchyard, and did not look back.

CHAPTER THREE

A DAY OR two passed, during which an autopsy on Hugo Montbray's body was performed. Local news reports informed viewers that it was hoped that the results would shed some light on what had happened to him, and showed a film montage of the Montbrays' Georgian home, standing stark and silent amidst wintry countryside, and police officers milling around Foxhay Brake. Then, to my surprise, Jake Fernsby flashed up on the screen, looking careworn and slightly uncomfortable in his work suit. His voice was a tense staccato as he repeated the known facts: Mr Montbray's death was the subject of ongoing investigations, and the police did not yet know what the cause of death had been or whether there had been any criminal activity in connection to it. The autopsy findings, he continued, would be crucial in determining exactly what had occurred.

Then, for a little while, there was a lull. The case apparently disappeared from the local media's output, and was rarely mentioned even in the village. The police cordons surrounding Foxhay Brake came down, and the paths were reopened for the joggers and walkers who wished to make use of them – which, by all accounts, most opted not to do. Even if Montbray's death had been nothing but a tragic accident, it still aroused a superstitious, almost primal, fear.

The sudden police and media silence did not surprise me, for I'd witnessed much the same thing before. It didn't mean that nothing was happening, only that nobody was yet able or willing to say much about it. Behind the scenes, I imagined, this was likely to be a frantically busy time, with journalists putting pressure on the police and the police, in turn, putting pressure on the Coroner's office. I found myself wishing, to my surprise, that I was covering the case too; but then I remembered my assurances to Jake Fernsby and my mother, and made no move to follow up on that wish. Still, my interest in the inquiry continued, and I spent several hours reading everything I could find about it.

I needed something to focus on, I suppose. Though the peace of Wintergreen was soothing, on another level it left me feeling restless. Perhaps I just had too much time to think. In London, I was always chasing some story, and I found that concentrating on other people's lives absolved me of having to worry too much about my own. Now, without that vital distraction, I found my thoughts turning to things I'd prefer to forget – my divorce, primarily, and the fact that, for a woman in her thirties, I had very little to call my own. Many of the people I'd gone to school with had homes and families and steady careers by now. I, on the other hand, was a childless divorcee who lived alone in a rented flat and didn't even have much of a personal life, just work and exhaustion and a haunting fear that life was slipping away.

One night, hoping to bring on the sleep that often eluded me, I took a short walk around the farm. It was a cold, clear night, and the stars above my head looked like tiny slivers of ice. I walked down the lane that led to the B road, which was still and silent at this late hour. Then I turned back and made my way across the farmyard towards Stable Cottage. The farmhouse loomed up before me, silhouetted against the sky. It was quiet at this hour, its windows dark, and I imagined that, if Lita was at home, she had gone to bed.

A step sounded somewhere in the farmyard, and a torch beam split the night in two. It swung around and came to rest on me. I narrowed my eyes against the sudden glare, and my heart gave a frightened thump in my chest.

"Oh, thank God," someone said, and I relaxed, recognising Lita's voice. She emerged from the shadows near one of the barns, and the torch beam fell away from my face. As she came towards me I saw that she was casually dressed in faded jeans and a quilted jacket, and for once appeared rather unkempt. No make-up, lank hair held back by a butterfly clip – she looked tired and worn, and older.

"I'm sorry," she said. "I hope I didn't alarm you. I heard footsteps out here, and came out to investigate. Just a precaution, you know. This area may look peaceful, but there have been quite a few break-ins in recent months. Farms seem to be especially vulnerable."

Now that I was closer to her, I could see that her eyes were red and inflamed, as if she'd been crying.

"What's wrong, Lita?" I asked.

She hesitated, as if wondering how much to tell me. I sensed that some strong emotion was warring against her customary outer calm. Then a tear leaked from her eye, and she brushed it away with an impatient hand.

"What's *right* at the moment?" she said in a strangled voice. "It's almost Christmas, and I'm alone here. I miss my husband. I miss my daughter. I'm exhausted, and I'm upset by what's been going on around here, in the village."

"What do you mean?"

"Hugo Montbray's death, for a start. I suppose you've heard about that?"

I nodded. "Did you know him?"

"Better than most, perhaps. He was my business partner – and my friend too, I suppose." She sniffed, and attempted to smile. "I sometimes think I must be jinxed, you know. The moment I form a connection with someone, something bad happens to that person."

I thought of her daughter, and wondered why she wasn't home for the holidays. Lita had said that she was at university, but the term should have finished by now. I shivered in the cold air, and glanced across at Stable Cottage, where a light shone in the window. I touched Lita's shoulder.

"Look," I said, "it's much too cold to stand around out here. Do you want to come inside for a drink?"

Inside, Stable Cottage was warm and suffused with a soft light. A fire burned low in the hearth, and my open laptop cast a ghostly light over the room. Lita flopped down onto the sofa, wiped her tears away, and gave me a brave, watery smile.

"Tea, or something stronger?" I asked.

"Definitely something stronger."

"I've got wine or brandy."

"Brandy's fine."

I rummaged around in the kitchen cupboards, and poured some brandy into two small glasses. She took a small sip, closed her eyes, and nodded.

"I could get used to this," she said. "A bit too easily, actually. I don't usually drink a great deal; you can't when you're running a business singlehandedly and you have to get up at five o'clock in the morning to go through the accounts or sort out some paperwork. It's terrifying sometimes: I have employees relying on me, and sometimes I wonder if I can even rely on myself."

"You're doing a fantastic job, as far as I can see."

She smiled, a little sadly. "It's not a job I ever imagined I'd be doing. I was an illustrator at one time, when my husband was alive, but I didn't make much money out of it. After he died, I had to put it aside in favour of something that would pay the bills. I didn't have much choice."

"I'm sorry." I sat down opposite her. "Did you ever resent that?"

"Of course. But I had my daughter to look after, so I did it anyway. The farm wasn't very profitable back then, you know. It was just after the foot-and-mouth outbreak in 2001, and we'd been badly affected around here. I needed to raise some money urgently, which was where Hugo Montbray came in. He looked at this place and saw what no one else could see. He suggested that I sell off a bit of land, and then convert some of the outbuildings into holiday homes and rental properties. He helped a great deal." She took another sip of brandy. "This is going to sound incredibly selfish, but now that he's gone I don't know what's going to happen. I don't even want to think about it."

"I'm sure you'll manage," I said, and then added, as gently as I could, "You obviously had a high opinion of him."

Lita, who was no fool, looked up and gave me a wry smile. "Unlike most people, you mean."

"That's what I've heard."

"You're not used to village life, Cat. Gossip gets repeated and embroidered, and wild rumours fly around. There's jealousy, rivalry. I'm not going to sit here and tell you that Hugo was a saint, but – well, people exaggerate. He knew what he'd done, and I knew what he was like. Either way, he's dead now. Death cancels all accounts."

"I've heard that the Montbrays don't have a particularly good reputation around here."

"Local folklore. Some of the Montbrays might well have been rogues, but people blow things out of all proportion. I suppose you've heard about the Montbray curse?"

I smiled. "I've heard a little bit about it, yes."

"It's one of those stories that tend to crop up time and time again. According to the story, one of the Montbrays seduced a local girl back in the dim and distant past. He ditched her when he'd had enough of her, and the girl – Patience, they say her name was – hanged herself. Of course, she found time to place a curse on the family before she went, condemning the male Montbrays to deaths as violent and premature as hers. Needless to say, the whole thing is nonsense. There's no historical evidence that such an event ever occurred, and many a male Montbray has lived to a ripe old age and died peacefully in his bed. Still, it gives people something to gossip about." She glanced at me, looking vaguely troubled. "Are you at all superstitious, Cat?"

"I cross my fingers sometimes, but in general, no."

"Then you won't be too alarmed to learn that Patience was supposedly a servant at this farm, and that she hanged herself in the stable – here."

Outside, a low wind sprang up and cried softly as it blew around the eaves. I blinked. Folklore or not, the idea of someone having killed herself in the very place where I was staying was a disconcerting one.

"Of course," Lita added, seeing my expression, "it's just an old story."

"Well," I said, recovering, "people need stories. And if I were the nervous type, I wouldn't have lasted long in journalism."

"I can imagine," Lita said, and smiled. The brandy appeared to be making her mellow, allowing her to forget her sadness. "Anyway, I've been living on the farm for years, and in all that time I've never been troubled by the supernatural. Lord, that might actually seem like a holiday compared to all the *natural* problems I've had to deal with: sick animals, money troubles, loneliness. Loneliness – oh, I've learned a thing or two about that, I can tell you. I feel it most at this time of the year."

I hesitated. "What about your daughter? Isn't she coming home for Christmas?"

"She's spending Christmas and New Year in France with some college friends. A whole group of them are going skiing together. I didn't have the heart to refuse her. Bethany had quite a lonely childhood out on this farm, and spending time with her friends means the world to her." She took another sip, and then reached into her jacket pocket and took out a wallet. Leafing through the different compartments, she took out a small photograph, which she handed over to me.

It was an ordinary snapshot, showing a teenage girl sitting at a table and smiling at the camera. A birthday cake stood before her, its candles glowing. The girl was small, with an elfin face, a rather mischievous grin, and fine blond hair that fell in loose waves to her shoulders – not pretty, exactly, but with the kind of sparkle and vivaciousness that sometimes counts for far more than simple prettiness. She was, I thought, the kind of girl who'd stand out in a crowd.

"What's Bethany studying?" I asked, handing the photograph back.

"Modern languages. She wants to be a translator or interpreter when she's older." Lita smiled. "She's always had such dreams, you know. She wants to move to London or New York, work for the UN perhaps. And the thing is, she has the ability. She has such a good brain. She was usually top of the class at school, and she didn't even have to work that hard to get there. She was wasted on a farm in Wintergreen, and I often wished I could have given her something different, something better." She finished her brandy, and put her glass back down on the table. "But she survived, and so did I. And in the end that's all that matters, isn't it?"

"I suppose so."

"And we'll keep on surviving." She glanced down at her watch, and stood up. "Thanks for listening to all my nonsense, Cat."

"It wasn't nonsense. And you're welcome."

"I'd better be going, anyway. Early start tomorrow – as usual. Goodnight, Cat."

"Goodnight."

I heard her footsteps echoing around the farmyard as she walked away, and then they faded, leaving only silence. I sat quietly on the sofa, finishing the brandy, looking around and seeing my surroundings with new eyes. I didn't really believe the story of Patience and the Montbray curse, of course — but sometimes such stories, however distorted, do contain a kernel of truth. I looked up at the beams above my head. Did a seduced, abandoned girl really hang herself there?

We choose to believe that the past is dead — we have to believe it, perhaps, if we're not to go mad. But what if time doesn't run along a comforting straight line? What if it turns back on itself? What if the moments we believe to be fleeting are in fact eternal, and the past never dies?

"If you're here, Patience," I said, "I'm sorry about what happened to you."

There was no reply. I hadn't really expected any. I shook my head, got up, and took the empty glasses over to the sink.

CHAPTER FOUR

I DROVE OVER to Alverston the next day, feeling strangely nervous. This was the town where I'd spent much of my childhood, where I'd gone to school, fallen in love and had my first job, but I hadn't seen the place in a long time. What if it had changed so much that I could barely recognise it? I'd be like a refugee from the past, washed up on the shore of an incomprehensible present.

I was relieved, then, when I drove into the town and saw that such changes as had occurred had taken place slowly, and that it was much the same as I'd remembered. As I parked the car and walked into the crowded town centre, I had a feeling that I was coming home. I'd never thought much of the place when I was growing up there, and had left as soon as I could, but none of that seemed important now. It had claimed a place in my heart before I'd even known it was there.

The town centre was gaudy with Christmas decorations, the shops overrun with people buying gifts. I wandered around for an hour or so, picking out some presents for my nephews and wondering what on earth kids liked these days. Finally, having bought one or two things that I hoped they wouldn't turn their noses up at, I sat down in a café and called Lorna. She answered at the fourth rung, and her rather impatient tone softened when I greeted her.

"*Cat!*" she said, as if she couldn't imagine it being anyone more wonderful. "Are you back for the holidays?"

"In Alverston as we speak. Do you want to meet up?"

"If it gets me out of this office for an hour or two, count me in. It's crazy in here." In the background, I could hear a low stream of chatter, punctuated with the shrill ringing of telephones. "How about the Sun in Splendour, half-past twelve?"

"Sounds good to me."

The Sun in Splendour, a pub just to the north of the town centre, had been a favourite of ours when we were younger. Walking in five minutes before I'd arranged to meet Lorna, I found that, like the town, it hadn't changed a great deal. It had always been a relaxed place, the kind of pub where drinking was secondary to eating and talking. I ordered some cider for both of us, and then sat down at a table in the corner. Around me, the lunchtime crowd were just starting to trickle in. "Baker Street" blared over the loudspeakers, a reminder of an innocent time when I'd seen London as the Promised Land.

I sipped my cider, wondering what effect time had had on Lorna. She had been one of my best friends in school, and we'd both shared an early interest in journalism. While other girls were chasing boys or experimenting with make-up, we'd written articles for the school newsletter and submitted pieces to the local paper, most of which had been politely rejected. Once we'd reached college age, though, our paths had diverged. I'd gone to London and, under the false impression that bigger was necessarily better, had aimed for the very top: the best publications, the best stories, everything. Lorna had been different. She'd stayed at home, found a junior position in the offices of the local paper, and worked her way up to the position of sub-editor. I sometimes wondered whether she hadn't done rather better than me, when all things were taken into account. In London, I was just one more hustling newshound. Here, Lorna enjoyed both authority and professional security, two things which had so far eluded me.

She arrived promptly, as she always had, looking rather more like an art teacher or mature student than a journalist. She'd put on weight over the years, and had taken to dressing in long skirts, jackets and biker boots. Her hair was coloured a vivid shade of red, and a small stud gleamed in her nose. She swept into the pub with the assurance of a woman who knows her place in the world, and gave me a hug.

"You look wonderful, Cat," she said as she sat down. "Have you been dieting?"

"Not really, no. I've just been too busy to eat – quite literally, on a few occasions."

"Still freelancing?"

"Yes." I smiled, shook my head. "The funny thing is that I thought it would be a more relaxed lifestyle, but in fact I can't remember the last time I had a day off. Even having an evening off seems like a luxury these days. Now that I'm here for the holidays, I don't know what to do with myself."

"Well, you certainly won't find many stories around here," Lorna said, examining the menu. "We just take what there is and stretch it as far as it will go. Not that we're any less busy because of that. It's a sad thing, but I sometimes think that the news, print or online, is just a vehicle for advertising these days. That's where most of our revenue comes from, anyway. What are you having, by the way? Please don't say salad. You need to bulk up a bit."

While Lorna was at the bar placing our order I remembered the Montbray case. I'd never really forgotten it, actually, only pushed it to the back of my mind.

"Oh yeah," Lorna said when I asked her about it. "The Montbrays are a big deal in these parts, Hugo in particular. He had an iron grip over the local real estate market, and dabbled in a lot of other things besides. Some of them, by all accounts, weren't entirely legit. There were rumours of fraud and the like, none of which anyone has been able to confirm, but which seem too widespread and consistent to be just malicious gossip. He made a lot of enemies, by all accounts. Even his own brother disliked him."

"Charles?"

"Yes. Works at the Town and Shire Bank, here in Alverston. He had some big bust-up with his brother shortly after their father died. Charles was adamant that Hugo had cheated him out of some of his inheritance. Again, it couldn't be proved. Hugo could afford the best lawyers, and I'm afraid that counts for a lot." Lorna shook her head and looked momentarily mystified. "For some reason, Charles has never moved out of the family home in Wintergreen. Perhaps it's stubbornness."

"Or perhaps it was a way of punishing his brother." I drank some more cider, waiting for the feeling of warmth it gave to kick in. "They're quite a family, aren't they? I've heard that Hugo was fond of women, too."

"Not *fond* of them, exactly." Lorna gave an utterly humourless laugh. "He wanted them, certainly. He loved and left quite a few girls, and broke a few hearts. One of them actually turned up in our offices a few weeks ago, believe it or not."

"Really?"

"Yes. A beautiful woman, late twenties, long blond hair. Sylvia Tatlow, I believe her name was. She claimed that she'd been having a passionate affair with Hugo which had gone sour, and she was out for revenge. She wanted to expose him in the papers, which was really quite sad; she seemed to be under the impression that this would constitute big news. We had to tell her, tactfully, that her story wasn't exactly the Profumo affair, that our paper wasn't a tabloid, and that we certainly weren't going to publish one person's unsubstantiated claims."

I stared at her. "She must be under a certain amount of suspicion at the moment," I said.

"That doesn't count for much, since she's hardly the only one. You see, Cat," – she leaned a little closer to me – "people are already speculating that Hugo's death might not have been an accident. Unlikely as it may sound, it perhaps wouldn't be altogether surprising if someone had – well, helped him on his way, let's say."

"You say that people are speculating. Would they include the police, by any chance?"

"Whatever the police think, they're not prepared to say much yet. If you ask me, though, they have their suspicions. They certainly don't seem to be in a great hurry to rule anything out. This hasn't been reported yet, Cat, but the initial findings of the autopsy are in. Hugo received a traumatic brain injury – an epidural haematoma, to be precise – probably from hitting his head against a rock when he fell. That would have been enough to kill him – eventually, at least. He appears to have remained alive for a short time afterwards, though he was probably unconscious. Some water was found in his lungs, so the immediate cause of death was drowning. But – and this is quite interesting – initial tests suggest that there was only a very slight amount of alcohol in his blood, consistent with, say, a small shot of liquor. It wasn't really enough to impair his coordination or dull his senses."

"Is there any reason to think he might have been taking any other substances?"

"Certainly not. He wasn't the type."

"And have you found out anything else?"

"Nothing that the police are willing to share with us just yet."

I thought of Foxhay Brake, or at least the little I had seen of it so far. Though a wooded area, it was not particularly wild or remote.

On the contrary, it was a place where local kids went to play and people walked their dogs. That, at least, was what it was like during the daytime. Why would anyone go out there after dark, though?

"What time did Hugo die, roughly?" I asked.

"The autopsy places his death somewhere between four and five o'clock on the evening before he was found. That's consistent with eyewitness reports. Hugo's mother last saw him alive at around four o'clock that evening, when it was just beginning to get dark, and the body was found at half-past nine the next morning." She drummed her fingers against the table. "I can't for the life of me work out why anyone would go for a walk in the woods just as it was beginning to get dark. There's no lighting out there, nothing; you wouldn't be able to see a foot in front of you when you were amongst the trees. It was out of character, in any case; he wasn't the type of person who had much of an appreciation for nature or enjoyed taking strolls in the woods. If all of this seems odd to us, Cat, then you can bet that the police are looking into it very closely."

"I've already met one of them," I said. "Detective Inspector Jake Fernsby."

Lorna gave me a sharp little glance. "Are you chasing a story, by any chance?"

"No. I'm not going to muscle in on your territory, Lorna. I just happened to meet him while we were both hanging around Foxhay Brake on the day Montbray's body was discovered."

"He's got ESP when it comes to reporters. He probably had you sussed from the beginning." She laughed. "I wouldn't be surprised if he was hanging around just to keep an eye on you."

"I get the feeling he doesn't hold journalists in particularly high regard."

"It's nothing personal. He's wary of us on a professional level, but he's also learned how to play us. He makes use of us when he needs us, but if he doesn't we're lucky to get a word out of him. Either way," Lorna added, with a meaningful glance, "he's a decent enough fellow, if you don't tread on his toes. And if you're really not intending to get involved in the case, you probably won't do that."

When we'd finished lunch we walked back to the town centre together, and made plans to meet again before Christmas. Lorna was hosting several parties, she told me, from rather formal and restrained affairs to hedonistic blowouts. She invited me to one of the latter.

"You might as well have a bit of fun while you're here," she said, "and believe me, we know how to have fun out here in the sticks. We'll put your London shindigs to shame."

"I bet you will," I said. "I've already worked out that this area isn't nearly as quiet as I thought it would be."

We turned into the car park where I'd left my car, not far from Lorna's offices, when she suddenly leaned closer to me.

"Don't make it obvious that you're looking," she murmured, "but this is Charles Montbray now, coming towards us."

I looked, and saw a rather young, rather tall man approaching from the opposite direction. He was more slender than his brother, if the photograph I had seen of Hugo was anything to go by, and not quite as self-assured. His expression lacked the arrogance I had seen in his brother's face, and his eyes blinked nervously behind thick glasses. Yet I saw something else, too. Beneath his mild facade, Charles Montbray was stressed, perhaps angry. His shoulders were tensed, and a nervous tic twitched his left eye. He walked past us without a word, but I thought I saw recognition in his eyes when he glanced at Lorna.

I waited until he was out of earshot, and then whispered: "If Hugo Montbray really was murdered, surely Charles must be a prime suspect."

"I think so," Lorna said. "I think he knows it too, which is probably why he looks so edgy. I mean, he ticks so many boxes: he had a definite connection with the victim, he had a grudge against him, and he knew his habits. The police must be taking an interest in him."

"He looked like he recognised you."

"I'm sure he does. The staff of the local paper aren't exactly his favourite people. His family have featured in our pages on a few occasions, and usually not in a very flattering way." She shivered. "I wouldn't want to upset him, would you? He might have been the underdog compared to his brother, but he's still a Montbray."

"I've absolutely no intention of upsetting him."

Lorna looked at me steadily. "You'd better not, Cat. Believe me, it wouldn't be worth it."

ON MY WAY back to Stable Cottage, I stopped at Foxhay Brake. I parked in the gravel space that had been filled with police vehicles the last time I saw it, and walked into the woods. The trees looked dense and mysterious in the dim afternoon light, and faintly sinister. I couldn't imagine coming here at dusk or after dark. Why had Montbray done so?

I followed the path, which cut through the heart of the woods and then emerged beside a stream. Bare branches dripped with rainwater, and the birdsong and sound of running water seemed muted and dull. The path suddenly rose in a steep incline, and when I reached the top I looked down. A sheer, rocky slope ran down to the stream, about ten feet below. The undergrowth around here had been trampled down, and a broken length of police cordon hung from a tree trunk. I felt that this was probably the spot where the police had recovered Montbray's body, though there were no other visible signs of his death. It would not be long before every last trace of what had happened here was erased.

I stood looking down at the sudden drop and the rocks beneath. I tried to imagine what it would be like to fall, to see branches spinning above your head and the rocks and water getting closer . . .

But, I reflected, it was not a fall that would necessarily result in death. Depending on how and where you landed, you might get away with a couple of broken bones; if you were lucky, you might not be seriously injured at all. Hugo Montbray had been spectacularly unfortunate. But as a method of either suicide or murder it wasn't dependable at all; there were just too many variables, too much that was left to chance.

It had to be an accident, that was all. An odd one, admittedly, and one that in many respects seemed to make little sense. Arbitrary, just as life and the world often seem to be.

I walked a little farther along the path, which suddenly veered off at a right angle. A small wooden bridge crossed the stream and the path continued on the other side where, I imagined, it led all the way up to the B road. Straight ahead there was a large fence with a PRIVATE PROPERTY sign prominently displayed on an iron gate. Peering through the trees, I could just about make out the Montbrays' Georgian house. Hugo had died just a few metres from his own back garden.

I shivered and, turning away, began to walk back. I didn't want to be in that place of death any longer. I kept my eyes on the ground so that I wouldn't have to look at the woods, or the naked branches that seemed almost to be reaching out to me.

Something glittered and caught my eye. I stopped and crouched down, and saw a round piece of glass. I looked more closely, and saw that it was a wristwatch, damp and smeared with mud, but with the hands still moving, relentlessly keeping time. I took a handkerchief out of my coat pocket and carefully picked it up, making sure that I didn't touch it directly.

It was, I saw, a striking watch, with a dark blue dial and gold astrological motifs, and an adjustable leather strap. The name of a famous, and expensive, designer was printed across the dial. Its size and design made me think that it was a ladies' watch, and probably an expensive one at that. It was not, at any rate, the kind of thing that would be carelessly lost or discarded in the woods – and yet that, apparently, was what had happened.

I stood up and looked around. In all likelihood, I thought, it had nothing to do with Montbray's murder. It was far more probable that someone had simply and innocently mislaid the watch while they were taking a walk out here. Still, something about its presence made me wonder.

I slipped the watch into a plastic bag that was in my pocket, and decided to take it to the police station in Alverston the next day. Whether it was innocent lost property or something more sinister, the local police officers would probably know what to do with it. I took one final look around, and then walked back to the car.

CHAPTER FIVE

I MEANT TO drive over to Alverston the next day, a Saturday. As it happened, though, when I called at my mother's house that morning I found Jake Fernsby sitting in the living room sipping tea, and looking for all the world as if he'd lived there for years. I felt momentarily surprised, and then remembered my mother's great gift for hospitality. Even when Adam and I had been young, and she was working all the hours God sent to support us, she'd always been ready to welcome one of our school friends for dinner or a sleepover. As I peered into the room, I saw that she'd even made some biscuits, and had persuaded him to eat some.

"Don't look so worried, Cat," she said when she saw my face. "Jake is not here in a professional capacity. He's helping to arrange the Christmas Fair this year, and is hoping to get our support."

I glanced at Jake, who shrugged and looked mildly embarrassed. I didn't know whether I was pleased to see him or not, even if his presence here seemed likely to save me a journey. In fact, I felt self-conscious and slightly annoyed, as if he'd forced his way into the private sphere of my family life.

"For heaven's sake, Cat," my mother snapped when I remained silent, "try to be hospitable for a change. Keep Jake company while I wash up. He might even persuade you to get involved."

"Not much chance of that," I grumbled, but I sat down anyway while Mum gathered up cups and plates on a tray and bustled out into the kitchen. The sound of the TV blared through the open door, making me think that Sam and Freddy must have taken refuge in there. Then the door closed, and there was a long moment of silence, which rapidly became oppressive.

"What kind of support are you looking for, exactly?" I asked at last.

"Anything that people are willing to give," he said, smiling a little awkwardly. "We hold the fair every year, and people just donate things they no longer want, which are then sold on. A lot of villagers use it as a chance to get rid of old junk. More often than not, we end up recycling unwanted presents from the year before. All the proceeds go to charity."

"It's a pity nobody told me before I came. I'd have given you some of the stuff that's clogging up my place back in London."

"You can help in other ways. You could volunteer to man one of the stalls. Or you could just turn up and buy something. Besides, your mother's offered to make some Italian cakes. You could help her, perhaps."

"I'm afraid I didn't inherit my mother's flair for cookery."

"Well, you could just help her to sell them on the night. You never know, you might even enjoy it."

"I don't see why I shouldn't give it a chance," I said, giving in. "I haven't got much else to do while I'm here."

"I'll bear that in mind." He leaned back in his chair, and I sensed that he was beginning to relax. "How are you enjoying your stay in the village so far?"

"It's very relaxing. Very quiet."

"So quiet that you've been carousing with a sub-editor from the local paper, I understand."

I stared. How had he known about that?

"I happened to speak to Lorna earlier today," he explained, seeing my expression, "and she mentioned that she'd met you. She said the two of you were old friends."

"School friends, originally. And I wouldn't say that going to the pub for lunch constitutes 'carousing', by the way. Do you often talk to her?"

"We have to talk, occasionally."

"Including about the Montbray case?"

His smiled faded, and his expression became guarded. "Perhaps. Why do you ask?"

"I went out to Foxhay Brake yesterday afternoon," I explained, "and I found something. It probably isn't relevant, but I was going to take it over to the police station today anyway."

I rummaged around in my handbag, and brought out the plastic bag in which I'd put the watch. He took it out and examined it for a moment, his face betraying no expression.

"Where exactly did you find this?" he asked at last.

"Between Montbray's house and the place where I assume his body was found."

"It doesn't necessarily mean much." He frowned over the watch. "This looks like a pretty good watch, though, not some cheap thing – a designer label, quite distinctive. Probably waterproof, given that it's still working after lying out in the open like that. Not that any of that is significant. As property prices go up, so more and more people find themselves being priced out of the market. These days, you need a bit of money to live in Wintergreen." There was a slightly bitter undertone to his voice, and I remembered what he'd said about being a local boy. Did he resent the moneyed newcomers? He put the watch back in the bag, and added in a more brisk tone, "It's probably just lost property. Thanks for handing it in, though."

"You're welcome."

He paused and looked at me. "You've clearly been taking something of an interest in this case," he said.

"I can't help but be interested. The moment something even remotely out of the ordinary turns up, I just have to follow it."

"Have you been talking to anyone about it?"

"I hardly know anyone around here. I spoke to Lorna, obviously, but apart from that I've only mentioned it to my family and my landlady."

"Your landlady being Lita McQuoid, I suppose."

"Yes. I expect you know her."

"Not well, but we're acquainted."

"She was quite upset about Montbray's death. She looked like she'd been crying. They shared some business interests, apparently."

"Crying?" He raised his eyebrows slightly. "That surprises me. Given how unpopular he was, I thought only his mother would be crying for him."

"Diana Montbray? I think I've seen her. She was in the church one evening. She looked quite weepy."

"Mrs Montbray spends a lot of time in church. In view of everything she's had to put up with, I suppose she could be forgiven for turning to God." He paused and looked out of the window, where a weak winter sun was shining. "Look, do you mind if we have a quiet word? Not in here. Perhaps we could go out for a walk."

Mystified, but curious, I went into the kitchen and made my excuses to my mother, and then followed Jake out into the quiet street. When we'd put some distance between ourselves and the house, he leaned a little closer to me and said: "Lorna tells me you're pretty well-regarded in London. She says you have rather a lot of contacts in the national press."

"You could say that. I'm a freelancer, and that involves having contacts all over the place."

"It all sounds very glamorous."

I laughed. "For the most part, it's like treading water. You run after any work that comes your way, struggle to meet deadlines, and get very little in return – certainly nothing in the way of loyalty or job security. But it's interesting, and no two days are ever the same."

"You know," he said, "Hugo Montbray's death hasn't really made much of an impact outside the immediate area. I think there were a few lines about it in one of the redtops, but apart from that, nothing."

"There's been no word yet as to whether the police are continuing to treat his death as suspicious. I think most people probably consider it more likely to have been accidental – which, as I'm sure you know, is generally considered far less newsworthy."

"Do *you* think it was an accident?" he asked pointedly.

"I don't know. All I can say is that, given what I've seen and heard so far, that seems to be the most probable explanation. At least," – I turned and looked directly at him – "I haven't heard anything to suggest otherwise."

He returned my gaze, his eyes cool.

"I thought you were just here to enjoy the holidays," he said.

"I am. I'm not really planning to write anything about this – unless, that is, it turns out to be the kind of story I just can't ignore."

He was silent for a moment, looking not at me but at the church tower in the distance. I thought these silences of his were probably deliberate, intended to baffle and unnerve. Years of questioning people, trying to extract information from them, had probably made him skilled at such tactics.

"I might as well be honest with you," he said at last. "I've had a somewhat troubled relationship with members of your profession in the past. Journalists haven't always been particularly helpful to me or my colleagues. Of course, being helpful is hardly your purpose, but the behaviour of some reporters has left a sour taste in my mouth. At other times, though, we've been able to work together quite well. They can cooperate with us to release facts to the public in a controlled manner, and lead public appeals for information. However, even local journalists tend to be absent from a place as small as Wintergreen. Most are based over in Alverston."

"Are you saying that you want me to help in some way?"

"After a fashion." He seemed to reflect for a moment, and then took a small card out of his pocket and handed it to me. I looked at it, and saw that it listed his official contact information: the police headquarters where he was based, an office number, a mobile number, and an email address. "People are sometimes reluctant to talk to the police. You, on the other hand – very few people in the village know you very well, or know that you're a journalist. They'll probably take you at face value, and they might also be rather forthcoming with you. Given your profession, I suspect you're quite good at getting people to talk. If you see or hear anything even remotely interesting about Montbray's death, or anything that might have a bearing on the case, I'd appreciate it if you'd contact me. In return, if this *does* turn out to be a big story, you'll have a head start on your colleagues when it comes to writing an exclusive."

"I see." I put his card in my pocket. "Given all you've just said, I suppose you think Montbray's death was due to more than a simple accident."

He gave me a sharp sideways glance.

"Everything that I'm about to say is off the record, Miss Armistead," he said. "If any of it leaks out, I'll want to know why."

"I won't tell anyone. And please, call me Cat."

"Okay, Cat. I'm sure you know how important this is. Controlling the flow of information can be a vital part of an investigation, as can a degree of misinformation."

"Of course."

"Well, then – Montbray. On the surface, as you say, his death looks like a textbook accident. A man goes for an evening walk after a glass of scotch or brandy, loses his footing in the oncoming darkness, and falls down a steep slope – not an especially large slope, but enough to injure or kill him, depending on how he falls. He's unlucky, hits his head, and dies. Anyone looking at it would think it was just a case of simple misfortune. But I can't help but feel that there was a little more going on that night than bad luck."

"Is there any evidence of foul play?"

"We're still waiting for the toxicology results, but so far we've no reason to think that Montbray drank a great deal or took any drugs. His work colleagues, his mother and even his brother all say as much. All Mrs Montbray will admit to is that he occasionally drank some scotch in the evening, just to wind down after work. It's also generally agreed that he didn't, as a rule, go out walking in the woods in the evenings. In fact, that's so far outside his usual habits that, in itself, it's fairly suspicious."

"He might have drunk a little more than usual that evening. It was a Sunday, after all.

And drink sometimes causes people to do things they wouldn't normally do."

"Of course, but there's more. Montbray had spent much of that day away from home, on business; he frequently worked at weekends, according to his family. He arrived back home just before three o'clock in the afternoon, complaining that he had a headache. Mrs Montbray says he went into the library at the back of the house, where he often went to unwind. She was in the parlour, which is nearby, when she heard him talking to someone."

"Did they have any callers that afternoon?"

"No one who came by the front door, certainly."

"Who was this other person? A man, a woman?"

"She can't say. She heard Hugo reply, though; he said something like 'All right, half an hour.' She assumed he was talking to someone on his phone, but then she heard the side door close. A few moments later she saw someone through the window, walking across the lawn, away from the house and in the direction of Foxhay Brake. She couldn't see much – it was beginning to get dark by then – just a figure in a thick coat and a hood. She couldn't even tell us whether it was a man or a woman. She says that Hugo came out of the library shortly afterwards. He didn't say a word to her, but she heard him put on his coat and leave by the side door."

"Where was Hugo's brother at the time?"

"A good question. He claims that he'd spent the afternoon walking in the countryside, but he doesn't have an alibi. He didn't return home until later, about five o'clock – or so he says. That isn't all, though. The pathologist has suggested that there were some signs of a struggle – a slight struggle that was over very quickly. There were some scratches on Montbray's body. His coat was torn, and some of his fingernails were broken. Some fibres were also found during the examination of the body. Initial tests suggest that they're a blend of acrylic and modacrylic polymers, the kind of thing that's often used in the manufacture of imitation fur. Montbray certainly wasn't wearing anything like that at the time of his death."

"Imitation fur," I repeated. "And the watch looks like a ladies' watch to me. Do you think a woman might be responsible?"

"Perhaps. There's no shortage of candidates, given some of Hugo's romantic escapades. But then again, perhaps not. The imitation fur might not have come from the murderer, but from someone he met earlier in the day. And the watch could be unrelated to his death."

"Lorna told me," I said, "that a woman was threatening to expose Hugo not so long ago."

"Sylvia Tatlow, I suppose." He shrugged. "Her name has come up. She had a reason to hate Hugo, certainly. Then again, she might just have been looking for publicity. She's an aspiring model, you know, and keen to get her face in the papers. She's not particularly choosy about how she does so, either."

We were silent for a moment or two. Our footsteps sounded heavy in the still air. The bell in the church tower chimed the hour, and a sudden pall of depression descended over me. People like my mother and stepfather came to live in places like Wintergreen, in part, because they believed them to be safe. In fact, the madness of the world just seemed to follow them there.

"One thing I don't understand," I said at last, "is why someone would try to kill Montbray *there*, like *that*. I saw that gully, Jake. You couldn't be sure that someone who fell down there would die as a result."

"What if it wasn't premeditated?" His voice was quiet, intense. "What if it was an argument that got out of hand?"

"Who would meet up in Foxhay Brake at dusk to have an argument?"

"Someone whose options were rather limited, perhaps. Someone who didn't have anywhere else to go. My feeling at this stage is that someone arranged to meet with him so that they could discuss something important, something private perhaps. They didn't want to be overheard, not even by their own families. Hugo lived with his mother and brother, so his house was out of the question.

They agreed to meet in Foxhay Brake, and at some point an argument flared up. The other person lost his or her temper, and there was a scuffle, in which Hugo either fell or was pushed over the edge of the gully. Quite possibly the other person did not intend to kill him, but when they saw what had happened they panicked and ran away. They didn't want to face a manslaughter charge and a possible prison term. But," he said, tapping the plastic bag containing the watch, "perhaps something got left behind."

"That's all just speculation."

"Of course, but speculating is just about all I can do at the moment. At any rate, I want to find out who this watch belongs to. Even if the owner had nothing to do with Montbray's death, they might have seen or heard something." He paused, gazing at the low hills that rose up to the north. "Look, will you come out to Foxhay Brake with me? I won't take up much of your time, but I'd appreciate it if you could show me whereabouts you found the watch."

Jake's car was parked outside his house, which was near the castle. It was a small house, quite old, made of red brick and fronted by a tiny, rather overgrown garden. I supposed he lived alone there now, and didn't have enough time to pull up weeds or mow the grass. His car, too, bore signs of a certain amount of neglect: mud spattered the paintwork, and the front passenger door had a dent in it. Inside, it was untidy. Paperwork and food wrappers littered the back seat, along with some clothes that had recently come back from the dry cleaners and were still covered in clear plastic. He had to move a blanket and paperback novel from the passenger seat before I got in. He might almost have been living in his car, which didn't really surprise me. Many journalists' cars looked much the same, perhaps because neither profession tends to be conducive to an orderly home life.

"Excuse the mess," he said, as if he'd read my mind. "I always seem to be on the move, going from one place to another. There are times when I hardly spend any time at home at all. Do you mind if I turn on the radio?"

"Go ahead."

He pressed a button on the dashboard, and lilting piano music filled the inside of the car. I wondered whether Jake Fernsby took refuge in music, as I often had. In the aftermath of my divorce, on those seemingly endless nights when sleep was impossible, I'd lain in the darkness surrounded by the strains of Bach, Mozart and Handel. At the time, I'd often been so absorbed in my own pain that I was blind to other people's sorrow. Now, sitting next to Jake, I remembered that there are far worse things than a divorce. Derek and I had parted by mutual agreement, and the end of our life together had also signified a new beginning. How must it feel, though, to lose a beloved wife and child, and on a single day? What did that do to you?

I glanced across at Jake. As far as I could see, he appeared to have come to terms with the past, but I knew from experience that people can be surprisingly good at concealing their pain. Some explosions take place deep underground, so deep that they are barely perceptible on the surface, and some wounds are no less serious for being hidden.

Foxhay Brake lay still and silent beneath a sudden burst of winter sunshine. Despite the weather, nobody else seemed to be out and about. Jake left the car in the gravel parking space, and we got out and walked together towards the woods. A keen north-easterly wind blew in, shaking branches and sending the last of the year's leaves dancing in front of it. We walked along the path, not saying much, until we reached the area where I'd found the watch. Jake crouched down and looked at the ground, and then looked back and forth along the path.

"You know," he said, "there were policemen and forensic investigators scouring these woods on the day Montbray's body was found. Either they didn't see the watch, or it just wasn't here then."

"I only saw it by chance. I just happened to see the glass dial shining. It was almost hidden by the undergrowth."

"I see." He stood up and frowned. "Let's assume, for the sake of argument, that the person who lost the watch was involved in Montbray's death. Given that you found it here, they must have either arrived from the direction of the Montbrays' house, or gone back in that direction afterwards, or perhaps both."

"That doesn't tell us much," I pointed out. "According to Diana Montbray, that person might also have gone to see Hugo shortly before he came out here. She saw him or her heading back in this direction."

"It all helps to build up a composite picture, though. I think this was a local person, someone who knew the area and knew where Montbray lived. Not many people outside Wintergreen are even aware that Foxhay Brake exists."

"Your number of suspects is very limited, then."

"Indeed." He gave a rather crooked smile. "Since a large number of them disliked Montbray, though, that doesn't necessarily help much."

"Do you think you can find the owner of the watch?"

"Perhaps. It may depend on whether the owner of the watch wants to be found." He paused, glancing around at the silent woods. "If you lose something hereabouts, the best place to look for it is usually in the local paper. There's a regular Lost and Found column. Villagers who come across lost property either ask around or leave notices in the village hall, or they hand it over to me – and I usually get in touch with Lorna's colleagues and ask them to put a line or two in the paper. If the owner does come forward, we'll have a chance to question him or her. If nobody responds – well, that might tell us something too."

"That that person doesn't want to draw attention to themselves, perhaps."

"Well, maybe. Whether somebody comes forward or not, though, it's not unreasonable to think that they'll be keeping an eye on the local paper in the days to come. If you'd committed a crime and had lost a personal possession near the crime scene, how would you be feeling?"

"Nervous, to say the least. Perhaps they've already been back here, looking for it."

Footsteps sounded farther along the path, coming from the direction of the car park. I looked around, startled, and saw a man wearing a windcheater and jeans heading towards us, with his hands in his pockets and his head down. He looked up as he caught sight of us, and I recognised Charles Montbray. We looked at each other, just for a second, and I thought his eyes hardened a touch. Then he glanced at Jake, and a look of apprehension crossed his face before his usual mild expression slipped back into place. He nodded at us, and then walked past without a word.

"Oh Lord," I said when he was out of earshot. "I think he recognised me. I saw him yesterday, while I was in Alverston with Lorna. Do you consider him to be a suspect?"

"Since he was the deceased's brother, and had a definite reason to hate and resent him, we can hardly rule him out. But then again, we've got no real evidence against him – or anyone else, for that matter." Jake frowned. "Be careful, Cat. If you've noticed him, he's probably noticed you too. You don't want to make enemies."

"He doesn't know who I am."

"He could probably find out, if he wanted to. If he knew you were a journalist, he might feel quite worried anyway – and now that he's seen you with me, God knows what he's thinking. I'm not saying he's actually dangerous – he's lived in this village since he was born, and he's never been in trouble, not even for a parking ticket – but you need to be careful."

"Why do you think he was out here today?"

"For any one of the number of reasons that people might be out here – to go back home from the village, perhaps, or just to get some fresh air. In and of itself, it's hardly suspicious behaviour."

But it might be, I thought, though I said nothing.

We began to walk slowly back towards the car park. A picture formed in my mind: a picture of someone else walking in these woods, glancing around furtively, not wanting to be seen. Looking down at the ground, trying to find the lost watch, fearing – with good reason – that even a small mistake could betray them. If Jake was right, and Hugo's death was not premeditated, the person responsible was not a cold-blooded killer. He or she would be anxious, distressed about what had happened, and frightened of the consequences.

"Not many people have been out here since Montbray died," Jake commented as we walked. "I suppose nobody wants to take any chances, even if they do believe that it was an accident. Perhaps there's a bit of instinctive superstition involved, too. Either way, it's not nearly as busy as it ought to be on a day like this. Normally, people would be passing through all the time, walking their dogs or taking some exercise."

"It's a beautiful place," I said, which it was – if you could forget what had happened there.

"And safe – or so we always thought, anyway. I used to come out here quite often, at one time."

I glanced at him out of the corner of my eye. His face was turned forwards, his expression unreadable. I wondered whether he'd once come here with his wife and daughter, and whether, when he looked at the place, he thought not of Hugo Montbray but of the people he'd loved most, and who were now lost. I wondered how he managed to go on living in a place with so many memories. Perhaps those memories comforted him, and lightened the shadows that hung over his life.

We arrived at the car park at last, and he drove me back to Willowgate Farm, largely in silence. I think his mind was on the case; he seemed, at any rate, to be lost in his own thoughts. As I was taking off my seatbelt, though, my hand brushed against his. It was the tiniest touch, over in a second, and I don't know why it affected me so much. But for a long time afterwards, the skin on my hand seemed to tingle and burn.

AS I WALKED across the farmyard, and as the sound of Jake's car retreated into the distance, everything seemed hushed; even the animals were quiet. I glanced around, but saw no trace of Lita or the farm workers. The farmhouse looked lifeless and still. I unlocked the door of Stable Cottage, made some tea in the kitchen, and then sat down with my laptop, meaning to do some work. I started with some quick Internet searches on Charles Montbray and Sylvia Tatlow. Of Charles, there were only the barest online traces: entries in telephone directories, and a brief mention on the website of the Town and Shire Bank in Alverston, where Lorna had said he worked. He seemed to have avoided social media, at least under his real name, and I got the feeling that he was a man who valued privacy and enjoyed his anonymity.

Sylvia Tatlow was another story. She was on every major social media site, and her contributions consisted mainly of photographs of herself. She was indeed a beautiful woman, as Lorna had said: tall and slender, with fine features and blond, silky hair. Many of the photos she'd posted looked like the work of professionals, and reminded me of what Jake had said – that she was an aspiring model, and fond of public attention. Her verbal communications centred on some rather dull revelations about her everyday life: where she'd gone on a particular day, and who she'd seen while she was there. Amongst all of this, though, I could see no references to Hugo Montbray. Perhaps she'd been relying upon the established media in her quest to shame and discredit him. I was left with the feeling that she was self-absorbed and vain – but none of that necessarily meant that she was capable of murder.

I put my laptop aside and sank back against the sofa. I felt drowsy – the sleepy pace of life in Wintergreen had a soporific effect, I found – and began to yawn. I stretched out, closed my eyes and fell into a deep sleep, in which there were no dreams, no sensations.

I don't know how much time passed. But when I awoke dusk was falling outside the window, and the cottage lay deep in shadow.

Something had disturbed me. I sat up, feeling my heart give a little skip, while goose flesh puckered the skin on my arms. I felt cold, though a fire still burned in the hearth, and uneasy. My eyes told me that no one else was there, but I knew that I was not alone.

The noise was faint and indistinct, so much so that I barely heard it at first. I sat still, listening. It was a woman crying, crying as if her heart was breaking. Her sobs sounded terrible, fractured, and spoke of a sorrow that could not be contained. My eyes flickered around the room, looking for the source of the noise and seeing nothing.

I don't know how long the crying lasted. It was probably over in seconds, but it felt like an age – an age during which I could do nothing but sit and listen. I wasn't frightened, exactly – there was nothing obviously threatening about the experience – but I felt chilled and miserable, as if the shadow of someone else's sorrow had fallen over me.

The sobbing faded away at last – retreated, in fact, as if whoever was responsible was walking slowly away. Then it was gone, and I was alone once more. The cold withdrew, along with the feeling of depression. I stood up, rubbing my arms, and looked around the room and out of the windows. Nobody was there, either inside the cottage or outdoors. Either the crying had come from someone who had no physical being, or it had existed only in my own mind. Neither explanation was particularly comforting, and neither was easy to believe – but one was certainly true.

I chose, for purely pragmatic reasons, not to believe that I'd imagined the whole thing. I had enough problems already, I decided, without having to question my own sanity. That, however, really only left one option.

Stable Cottage. Its unimaginative name betrayed its former use. According to village folklore, a girl called Patience had hanged herself there after being abandoned by one of

Hugo Montbray's ancestors. It was the kind of myth that was easy to scoff at. But what if it were true?

Patience. A woman who'd been hurt by another Montbray, centuries before. The family seemed to have a remarkable talent for using, angering and irritating people, and the years seemed to have done little to curb their destructive instincts. But could there be some other connection between the present and the past?

"Patience?" I whispered. "Are you here?"

There was no reply. I turned on the light and sat down on the sofa, thinking. I had never believed in ghosts, at least not in the sense of the spirits of the dead. But perhaps certain things lingered. Perhaps certain actions and emotions, extreme grief or joy, could leave a kind of psychic stain on a place.

According to the old story, Patience had committed suicide. It was an act of violence, albeit one that had affected only herself. Had there been another act of violence recently, involving another Montbray?

There was a long list of people who might have killed Hugo. Hugo's brother, who felt that he had been cheated out of an inheritance. Sylvia Tatlow, and the other women Hugo had seduced and left. The people who had been defrauded, cheated, wronged in some way.

But – if it had been a murder – it wasn't a planned, premeditated killing. It had been emotional and impulsive. The person who had met Hugo in Foxhay Brake had probably not intended to take his life, but they had argued and things had got out of hand. And disagreements over business don't generally provoke such strong emotions – it would be easier, and far less risky, to settle such matters in court. If somebody had killed Hugo, they had been motivated by something far more personal, and infinitely more painful. Love. Hate. Betrayal.

I remembered the broken-hearted sobbing I had heard. The past never dies. Perhaps it just repeats itself, ad infinitum, world without end. And if Patience really was here, perhaps she was trying to tell me something.

CHAPTER SIX

I T WAS CHRISTMAS week, and the normal pace of working life was beginning to wind down. Even Willowgate Farm seemed to be going through something of a lull. With the earth deep in its winter sleep, perhaps there was simply less to do. The farm workers turned up later than usual, and went home earlier; Lita seemed to retreat into the farmhouse, where I imagined she was kept busy with her paperwork. There were small signs of life: a blurred glimpse of someone drawing the curtains, the sound of piano music, smoke pouring out of a chimney. I remembered that Lita would be alone this Christmas, and felt sorry for her.

I was kept busy by my mother, who was making frantic preparations for Christmas. I was sent to Alverston to shop for gifts and food, and told to drive to the nearest city, forty miles away, where there was an Italian deli. I bought Panettone, smoked ricotta, candied fruit, and many of the other things that my mother continued to crave but had trouble finding in the local area. I went to a party organised by Lorna, got a little drunk, and ended up sleeping in her spare bedroom. I woke up the next morning dressed in the clothes I'd been wearing the night before, smelling of drink and cigarette smoke and feeling rough.

In spite of all these distractions, though, I couldn't forget the Montbray case. And I found, to my annoyance, that I couldn't forget Jake Fernsby either.

In the miserable days following my divorce, I'd sworn to myself that I'd never get involved with anyone again. For a while, I'd managed to live by that vow. In London I was surrounded by attractive, like-minded men, and rarely felt so much as a twinge of romantic interest in any of them. I hadn't been out on a date for years, and didn't feel that I was missing out on much. Having learned a very hard lesson in the value of self-reliance, I wanted to build a future that was mine alone, and depended on no one else. Besides, I was consumed by my job, to the extent that everything else sometimes seemed inconsequential. Men had, for a very long time, been the last thing on my mind.

I had no idea why I was drawn to Jake when so many others left me cold. It was infuriating, not least because there couldn't possibly be any future in such an attraction. Jake belonged here in Wintergreen, and was probably still dealing with the after-effects of bereavement. I could no more imagine settling down here than I could imagine him moving to London. It would be better, I thought, to just take these weeks for what they were – a diversion, a distraction from the ongoing business of my life.

Hugo Montbray's funeral took place that week. I watched from a discreet distance as a hearse drew up before the village church and a group of undertakers lifted a coffin onto their shoulders and carried it through the gate. Following close behind were a small knot of mourners, including the woman I had seen at the church before, Diana Montbray. She clung to the arm of a woman who might have been a sister or friend, and dabbed at her face with a handkerchief. Behind her was Charles Montbray, dry-eyed and apparently unmoved. He looked in my direction, and I shivered despite the distance between us.

I wondered how much the police had told the family. I imagined that Jake had been to see them personally at some point, but I had little idea what he would have said to them. Had he told them that he believed that someone had killed Hugo? Did they already guess, or know? Had he questioned Charles, and tried to draw the truth out of him?

"Did you know him?"

The voice, high and quavering, startled me. I turned my head and saw a woman standing near me – a young woman, with long blond hair and large, beautiful blue eyes. There were no tears in those eyes; in fact, they glittered with a lively emotion that looked remarkably like excitement.

"No," I replied. "I just – well, I've been staying here in the village. Mr Montbray's death has been a big shock to people around here."

"Not as much of a shock as it would have been to him," she said. "He would never have seen it coming. He thought he was immortal."

"I suppose you knew him, then."

"Very well." The woman gave an odd, bitter smile. "In the Biblical sense of the term too, at one point. I was a fool, and he had no conscience."

All at once I realised who this was: Sylvia Tatlow. The woman Lorna had mentioned, the woman who had threatened Hugo with exposure. She looked slightly different in the flesh – a little less tall, and rather less polished – but it was certainly her. And far from being upset at Hugo's death, she seemed to be revelling in it. As she gazed at the church, a cruel smile marred her lovely features, distorting them horribly.

"I'm sorry," I said, not knowing what else I could say.

"I'm not," she replied. "It was a slap across the face, but sometimes that's what you need. I won't be in a hurry to give my heart away again. And I'm not sorry that he's dead. The only thing I *do* regret," she added, "is that I didn't send him on his way."

Didn't you? I thought. I didn't have time to question her further, however, for no sooner had she said these words than she had turned away and walked down the street with a quick, impatient stride. I gazed after her retreating figure. Physically, she was rather slight, which in itself made me doubt whether she could have killed Hugo; but she certainly had a motive, and perhaps anger can lend strength. She was smartly dressed, in clothes that looked new and expensive, and I remembered the watch I had found in Foxhay Brake. I could imagine her buying and wearing such a thing.

But then, I thought, if she *had* killed Montbray, would she really show up at his funeral like this? Would she talk about how much she had hated him, and how she wished she had hastened his death in some way? I had the sense that she was an uncomplicated woman, honest in her own way, and incapable of hiding her emotions. She didn't seem sly or deceitful enough to be a murderer – but that was just a feeling, and maybe not a very reliable one.

She turned into the churchyard and then marched along the path towards the door. I watched, wondering whether she intended to burst into the church and make a scene, but instead she simply stayed at the door, apparently listening to the service that was taking place inside.

I took out my phone and sent a message to Jake. My encounter with Sylvia had not amounted to much, but he'd asked me to get in touch if I saw or heard anything relating to Hugo's death. He replied a few minutes later, and his message was terse: "V interesting. Let me know if you see anything else."

For the time being, though, I decided that I really didn't want to see any more. I put my phone in my pocket, turned away, and left

Sylvia Tatlow and the Montbrays and all the rest of them to their grief, or guilt, or whatever else they might have been feeling.

THERE ARE ALWAYS things that can distract you, if you let them. One such thing occurred on the evening of Montbray's funeral, when I discovered that, even in recently refurbished properties, things are apt to break and fail with surprising regularity. Arriving in Stable Cottage that evening, I felt drained and grimy and in desperate need of warm water and soap. When I turned on the shower, however, I found that the water that came out remained stubbornly cold. Muttering to myself, I threw on an old pair of jeans and a sweater and made my way over to the farmhouse, hoping that Lita would be able to sort the problem out before Christmas. Taking cold showers in this weather would, I was pretty sure, lead to a bout of pneumonia.

There was no reply when I rang the doorbell. I rang a second time, waited, and then tried the door. It was locked, and I concluded that Lita must be out. As I walked back across the farmyard, though, I saw that one of the barn doors was wide open, spilling golden light across the dark cobbles. I thought that perhaps she was there, looking after a sick animal or attending to some other work, and so I made my way inside and looked around.

It was a large, high-ceilinged barn and, as far as I could tell, given over to the storage of farm equipment and bales of hay. As I peered around, though, I saw that nobody appeared to be there after all, which was strange – I could not imagine either Lita or one of her employees leaving the door wide open and the light switched on.

"Lita?" I called softly.

There was no reply, but I sensed something moving at the edge of my field of vision – a very slight, very quick motion. I turned around, feeling my heart stutter and then quicken, and saw a little flash of movement in the corner, where some hay bales were stacked up. It was barely there before it was gone, and for a moment I wondered if I had imagined it. Then I heard something: a tiny rustle and a crackle, as if someone were stepping on hay.

I quickly ran through the possibilities in my head. If it had been Lita there, she would have come out to meet me straight away – she was too old and too serious to be playing silly games. The same went for the farm employees, who all knew perfectly well that I was renting Stable Cottage, had seen me around the farm before, and would hardly hide like frightened children just because I showed my face in one of the barns. The only other possibility I could envisage was that I had disturbed a burglar. Lita herself had told me that there had been several break-ins in the area, many of them targeting farms, and I imagined that some of the machinery in the barn must be quite valuable.

I began to back out of the barn slowly, keeping my eyes fixed on the corner where I had seen the movement. I saw nothing else, but I sensed that someone was there, perhaps watching me as I went. As soon as I was out of the door, I turned and ran to Stable Cottage.

When I got back inside I bolted the door behind me, while my heart hammered and my breath came in short gasps. After taking a moment to get my breath back, I grabbed my phone and called the emergency services. An eerily calm operator listened to me, advised me to stay inside the locked cottage and wait, and told me that some police officers would be along as soon as possible.

The fifteen minutes or so that followed were some of the most tense and miserable of my life. I peered around the edge of the curtain to see if anyone was out in the farmyard, but I saw nothing. During one nightmare moment, I believed I heard light footsteps outside. I wondered if I had been, or still could be, in any kind of danger. Most burglars, if disturbed, simply ran away – or so I'd always been led to believe. Surely, though, there were exceptions . . . The police, I knew, would have to come all the way from Alverston, and wouldn't arrive for a while. I tried calling Lita, and left a message when there was no reply. Then, having exhausted all other possibilities, I called Jake.

He answered after six rings, sounding irritated – until I introduced myself.

"Stay where you are, Cat," he said when I told him what had happened. "Don't leave the cottage until the police arrive."

"I won't. I hope they get here soon, though."

"They'll be with you as quickly as they can." I heard him moving around, perhaps searching for clothes or shoes. "Hang on. I'll be there in a few minutes."

As it happened, he arrived at almost exactly the same moment as his uniformed colleagues from Alverston. No sooner had the police car driven up the rough farm track and lit up the night with flashes of blue light than Jake's plain car followed. I peered out of the window and saw him exchange a few words with the officers, who clearly recognised him. He glanced over and saw me at the window, and then came over to the cottage and knocked on the door.

"Can you point out the barn where you saw something?" he asked when I opened up.

"The large one over there," I said, pointing; and then I paused, surprised. "That's odd."

"What?"

"When I was there the light was on and the door was open. It's closed now."

"Okay. We'll go and have a look. Stay here."

I watched as they made their way over to the barn and opened the door. My senses were so heightened, my nerves so on edge, that I almost saw someone looming out of the shadows, almost heard the noise of a confrontation – but nothing happened. No sounds disturbed the night, and the officers appeared to encounter no resistance as they turned on the light and went inside. I waited indoors, wondering what had happened, what *was* happening. Five minutes later, Jake reappeared in the farmyard. I watched from the window as he walked over to the farmhouse. There was no reply when he knocked at the door, and he stepped back and looked up at the dark windows. Then he turned and came over to the cottage again.

"Are you okay?" he asked when I opened the door.

"I'm fine." Across the yard, I could see the officers coming out of the barn. "What did you find?"

"Nothing. There's no sign of any disturbance and, as far as we can tell, nothing has been taken. If there was an intruder, you probably frightened him away."

"*If?*" I repeated. The doubtful note in his voice riled me. "Somebody was certainly there earlier, and I'm pretty sure it was someone who had no business being there."

"Someone who turned out the light and closed the door as he left?" His voice was gently sceptical. "Forgive me, Cat, but isn't it possible that you allowed your imagination to run away with you?"

"I really don't think so," I snapped. "I'm not in the habit of seeing and hearing things that aren't there, and I'm not some little kid who gets scared if she's left alone after dark. Look, Jake, somebody was *there*. And I can't see why anyone who had a good reason to be there would hide from me like that."

"All right, all right." He held up his hands in a conciliatory gesture. "You were right to call the police anyway, just to be on the safe side. Have you tried to contact Lita?"

"Yes. I called her mobile number. There was no answer, but I left a message."

"You have no idea where she might be?"

"No, none."

"And you're sure that no one else is at the farm this evening? Workers, relatives, friends?"

"I shouldn't think so. As far as I know, the workers tend to leave by about six o'clock or so. Besides, the farmhouse is locked up, and nobody answered when I rang the bell earlier."

He paused and looked up at the dark shape of the farmhouse, and for a moment something – a doubt, a question – seemed to flicker in his expression.

"It's a strange old place, this farm," he said. "Centuries of history and a great many secrets. I don't know how Lita manages to live out here on her own."

"I think she manages pretty well," I said, surprised.

"That's the impression she gives, perhaps." He glanced at me, and suddenly he looked tired and older. "There are certain things that nobody really manages. You just learn to live with them somehow."

I guessed that he was talking about his wife and daughter, and I had no idea what to say to him.

I heard the low rumble of a car approaching along the lane, and a few moments later a pair of headlights tore through the night. As they drew closer, I realised that it was Lita's car. I caught sight of her pale, tense face as she stopped in front of the cottage.

"I got your message, Cat," she said as she got out. "What's happening here?"

"Nothing much," I said awkwardly. "I thought perhaps there was a burglar in the barn, but nobody's there now. I might have worried you for nothing."

"You did the right thing." She turned to Jake. "Did you see anyone?"

"Nobody was there when we arrived, Lita. If it was a burglar, then Cat probably scared him off. Strangely, there's no sign of any break-in."

"Quite possibly there was no need of one. Some of the workers here are quite young and inexperienced, and they're forgetful. Leaving a door open is the kind of thing they might do."

"Yes." He hesitated. "It's curious. Cat found the barn door open and the light on, but by the time we arrived, somebody had shut the door and turned the light off. Hardly the behaviour you'd expect of a burglar, is it?"

"I don't suppose it is, no. But people behave in all kinds of ways when they're under pressure. Perhaps he was trying to cover his tracks."

"Perhaps." He paused again, met her eyes for a moment, and then looked away. "Would you like to have a look around, Lita, and make sure that nothing has been taken?"

Lita set off across the farmyard with her quick, determined stride. I heard her exchange a few words with the officers before she went into the barn. Jake looked after her, saying nothing. The farmhouse hung over us, dark and silent. It was empty, I knew; and yet somehow it didn't *feel* empty. It felt heavy and unhappy and full of secrets, like a house that was not at peace. Another place where the past had never really died.

Lita reappeared in the farmyard after a minute or two, and made her way over to the farmhouse. She let herself in, and the lights flickered on, one by one. The uniformed officers were milling around, one talking into a radio and the other taking down some notes. I felt that they were getting ready to leave, and were perhaps slightly annoyed at having been called out here for nothing. And, I realised, it *was* nothing, after all. Whatever I had seen this evening, there was no evidence that it had been a burglar.

"It looks like I've wasted your time," I said to Jake. "I'm sorry."

"Don't be. It's always better to make sure in a case like this." He turned to look at me.

"Don't you ever feel nervous, Cat, being on your own out here?"

"Not particularly. Besides, burglars aren't usually dangerous, are they?"

"I wasn't just thinking of burglars. As I said, it's a strange old place."

I remembered the crying I'd heard, and was inclined to agree, but decided not to say as much. If he thought I'd been imagining burglars, God only knew what he'd think if I claimed to have encountered a ghost.

"It's a place with a history," I said. "I'm aware that it's associated with the old legend, the seduced maid and the Montbray curse. Is that what you're thinking of?"

"There may be a grain of truth in that old legend."

"Is this going to turn into a ghost story?" I asked, sounding rather more flippant than I felt.

He looked at me. "No. But perhaps you shouldn't be entirely dismissive of these things either."

"I'm not." I sighed. "Maybe I'm not dismissive enough. It certainly didn't take much to scare me tonight. I've a feeling I might have ruined your evening."

"I wouldn't say that," he said, meeting my gaze. "I wouldn't say that at all."

The farmhouse door slammed, and we turned to look. Lita had come back out, and was walking towards us again.

"No sign of a disturbance," she said, and smiled; but I could see the tension in her tight jaw and stiff shoulders. "Nothing's been touched, as far as I can see, either in the barn or in the farmhouse. It looks like you've had a wasted journey, Jake."

"No problem." He hesitated, very slightly. "This is a lonely place, Lita. If you're ever concerned about anything, don't hesitate to call us."

"Loneliness doesn't bother me. But thank you anyway."

"Will you be all right now?" Jake asked, and looked at me as he said it.

"We'll be fine," Lita said with quiet certainty.

"Okay then. Goodnight." He nodded at me, and our eyes met for a second. Then he went back to his car, switched on the engine, and drove slowly back down the track. He was followed a moment later by the police car.

Lita and I were left standing together in the dark, listening as the car engines faded into the distance. I glanced at her, and saw the tension in her face. Dark shadows ringed her eyes, and she looked pale. Unusually, her face was bare of make-up. I wondered what was wrong. Was it simply that her daughter wouldn't be with her for Christmas? Was it the memory of her dead husband? Perhaps she missed him most at this time of year.

"I stressed you out for nothing, Lita," I said. "I'm sorry."

"You did the best thing you could have done, Cat. If there was a burglar and you *hadn't* called the police, God only knows what might have happened." She looked at me. "Why were you out in the farmyard?"

I remembered the absence of hot water in the cottage, which I'd completely forgotten about in all the excitement. Lita frowned and rubbed her forehead when I told her about it, and I felt sorry to have presented her with yet another problem.

"Oh Lord," she said, "another thing to worry about. Well, don't worry, Cat. I'll call someone out tomorrow to take a look at the boiler. Can you do without hot water just for tonight?"

"Yes. Yes, of course."

"Okay." She seemed relieved to hear it. "Well, goodnight, Cat."

"Goodnight."

She turned and hurried across the farmyard, and I felt that she was anxious to get back inside.

I DIDN'T SLEEP well that night, which I suppose was hardly surprising. I wandered through confused dreams of dark houses, empty houses that were not empty at all. I dreamt of Jake's thoughtful gaze, and of Hugo Montbray stumbling through Foxhay Brake, never guessing that he had only minutes left to live. I dreamt of Patience, and of how she had paid the price for the Montbrays' heartlessness.

I was thirsty and hot. I threw off the covers, switched on the bedside lamp, and made my way out into the living room. What I saw there made me stop short, and my heart constricted painfully in my chest.

Someone was hanging from the ceiling beam: a small woman with untidy dark hair, wearing a long dress. A rope had been tied crudely about her neck, and her head was at an awkward angle. Her feet were bare, and urine dripped from her toes. I took a step towards her. She was dead; her eyes were glazed over, and her skin had a bluish tinge.

I cried out and stepped back; and then I awoke in my bed, with my pulse thundering. I reached for the bedside lamp, and golden light flooded the room. Just a dream. Oh thank God, just a dream . . .

But the movement at the window was not a dream. Someone ducked out of sight as I looked, and disappeared. I didn't catch any features, just the vague outline of someone's upper body. I sat still for a moment, listening to the whir of blood in my ears. Someone had been standing outside, peering through the curtains, which were slightly ajar. Who that person had been, and why they would be doing such a thing, I had no idea.

I got out of bed and crept across to the window. In my overheated imagination several nightmare scenarios played out: a hideous figure jumping out of the darkness at me, the glass smashing, a hand reaching inside . . .

But when I reached the window and looked out, I saw nothing but the darkness and the black shapes of the trees in Foxhay Brake. If somebody really *had* been there – and I felt certain that somebody had – they had melted away into the night, leaving behind nothing but questions.

If I had been in a braver mood, I might have gone outside to look around. But after everything that had happened – Montbray's death, the handful of curious experiences I'd already had, and the supposed burglary – I didn't feel nearly as bold as I normally would. I pulled the curtains across, and then went around the cottage, checking the doors, making sure that everything was secure. At last I made some tea, and sat down to drink it. I turned on the TV to drown out the silence, the sense of being alone – or not alone, perhaps.

Why would someone be peering through my bedroom window in the middle of the night? I didn't think there were enough people in Wintergreen for a stalker to be a serious possibility, and I'd hardly been there long enough to merit such attention anyway. I didn't have any enemies in the area, and there was nothing about my life that warranted such a level of interest. Some wandering deviant who enjoyed watching women as they slept? It hardly seemed likely – but what other explanation was there?

I shook my head. It was bizarre; it made no sense at all. And yet I had the feeling that somehow, somewhere, there was an underlying reason, a logic. It was just a question, perhaps, of finding out what it was; and though I was still afraid, the thought made my reporter's antennae twitch.

Whatever happened next, I thought, this would be a Christmas like no other.

134

CHAPTER SEVEN

THE VILLAGE HALL opened its doors at seven o'clock, and people began to arrive immediately – a trickle at first and then a torrent, until it seemed that almost everyone in Wintergreen and the surrounding area had turned up. Watching unobtrusively from the corner where my mother's stall had been set up, I thought that the Christmas Fair must be one of the big events of the village calendar, a chance for everyone to come together for some shared purpose. Those who weren't manning stalls were buying enthusiastically from them, probably stocking up on a few last-minute gifts. Christmas songs played over the sound system, and fake snow had been sprayed over the windows. A large tree stood in the corner, lights twinkling amidst its foliage.

My mother's stall was one of the big attractions, and I was kept busy helping her. She'd spent the past few days in the kitchen baking, and had made enough to get the entire village through a siege. There was citrus tart, Gianduia cake, Sicilian cassata and tiramisu, along with some of the spicy biscuits she'd made for my brother and me when we were kids. There were jars of homemade pesto and tomato sauce, and fresh ravioli. My mother, an exotic bird amongst plain English sparrows, was well aware of the impact she made, and she enjoyed it. I watched as she chatted and laughed and explained the basic principles of Italian cooking to her neighbours, and felt that she had finally found her place in the world. I was happy for her. It had been a hard-won victory.

"Exactly what are we raising money for?" I asked her, during a rare lull.

"A minibus to take people to Alverston for shopping and a day out once a week.

There isn't a regular bus service, and those who can't drive often find themselves becoming a little isolated." She nodded across the hall at Jake, who had just arrived and was talking to some stallholders near the door. "It was Jake's idea, and rather a good one too."

"He seems very devoted to the village," I said.

"It's his home."

"It must hold some pretty bad memories for him."

"And many good ones too, I think." She smiled, a little sadly. "He never talks about these things, of course, so I can only guess, but I think that being in the places he associates with his wife and daughter comforts him. Others of us find little such comfort, and the bad memories overpower us."

She was thinking, I knew, of my father's loss. The experience had haunted her so much that, in the end, she had simply moved away from the place where she had lived with him, and where Adam and I had been born. Our original home had been in the North of

England, far away from these soft meadows and gentle hills, amidst moorland and fells. I had been ten years old when my father vanished from our lives, and my loss had haunted me ever since – more, perhaps, than I cared to admit. When my mother had finally moved down to Alverston, it had come as a huge relief. The upheaval of moving to a new town and trying to make friends in a new school had hardly even registered with me. All that had mattered was that we had got away, and wouldn't have to live in the shadow of our loss anymore.

Now, though, I wondered what else I had lost along the way.

"I miss Dad," I said quietly, and my mother looked at me sadly.

"You don't really remember him, Cat," she said.

"You hardly ever talk about him."

"There are good reasons for that."

I turned away, partly to hide my irritation. Among the things that I remembered from those years, and the things that I'd pieced together since, I knew that my parents had not been getting on very well in the years leading up to my father's loss. I guessed that much of the fault had been his. But these things, these guesses and memories that were fading by the year, didn't amount to much. I wanted facts, which my mother always seemed reluctant to supply.

I made my way outside, pleading that I needed some fresh air, and found myself in a children's playground that had been financed by a previous year's fundraising drive. The night was raw, with a cold wind blowing in from the north. Stars glimmered against the black backdrop of the sky, while Christmas decorations twinkled in the village. I could hear the sounds of music and laughter from the nearby pub, and they were comforting. Then I thought of Foxhay Brake and Stable Cottage, and the web of mystery that seemed to extend around them, and I felt nervous again.

The door creaked open, and Jake emerged, his face pale beneath the overhead light. He started when he saw me, and then smiled.

"Aren't you cold out here?" he asked.

"I needed a bit of fresh air."

"Right." He looked a bit awkward. "I don't suppose you'll be too impressed if I smoke, then."

"I don't mind."

"Thanks." He took a packet of cigarettes from his pocket, lit up, and breathed out a cloud of smoke. "Filthy habit, I know, but we're all entitled to a couple of vices. That's my excuse, anyway. I always swear I'll give up one day."

"That's what I always say about wine and chocolate."

"I imagine that you were brought up to appreciate good food and wine. Your mother cooks like an angel." He smiled. "You're very similar to her, you know."

"Physically, I suppose I am." People had often said so – I'd inherited her dark hair and the curious sea-green eyes that are often found in Italy, and had frequently been described as "exotic". "I can't cook to save my life, though. I barely have time to eat in London."

"That sounds familiar." He frowned as he took another drag on his cigarette. "I worked up in Manchester for a few years, and you know what? I hardly remember anything of that time. It's just one big sleep-deprived blur in my memory."

"Is that why you decided to come back to Wintergreen?"

"The older I got, the more attractive that prospect became." He shrugged. "I liked the idea of being back in a place where crime consisted of parking offences and the odd break-in. That's what it's like around here, most of the time — or what it *was* like, at least."

Hugo Montbray, I thought. It would be a long time before the gloom caused by his death lifted. Nobody even knew how he had died yet, though I supposed the police were still digging away at the case. I'd read a few lines in the local paper just yesterday morning, in the Lost and Found section. They were terse and to the point — *Ladies' watch found in Foxhay Brake, Wintergreen* — followed by a number to call for anyone who wished to claim it.

"Has anyone come forward about the watch yet?" I asked.

"Not yet. I didn't really expect anyone to." I sensed that he was unwilling to say very much about it. "Has everything been quiet over at Willowgate Farm? I notice that Lita isn't here tonight."

"I asked her if she wanted to come, but she had some paperwork to deal with. Everything seems quiet at the moment." I hesitated, remembering the person I'd seen lurking outside my bedroom window. "Well, not *entirely* quiet, perhaps . . ."

He cut me off. "What do you mean?"

I told him what had happened. He listened, and then cursed beneath his breath and ground his cigarette beneath his heel. "Why didn't you tell me?" he demanded.

I looked at him, surprised.

"It didn't seem like such a big thing. I mean, maybe one of the farm workers was fooling around, or something like that."

"*Anything* out of the ordinary could be a big thing," he muttered. "You're right on the edge of Foxhay Brake in that cottage, Cat. If someone's sneaking around out there at night, I want to know about it. Don't you sometimes feel worried out there?"

"What am I supposed to be worried about, exactly? Ghosts or killers?"

"Both, perhaps." He put his hands in his pockets and looked up at the sky. "I've always thought of Willowgate Farm as being a haunted place, you know. Haunted by ghosts or just by memories, but perhaps that's the same thing in the end. There's the old story about Patience, of course, but its recent history hasn't been much more cheerful. Lita McQuoid's endured a lot. Her husband's death, having to look after her daughter while running the farm – she's been through quite a bit."

"She seems to have dealt with it pretty well."

"Perhaps that's the impression she gives, but I wonder. What happened with her daughter is enough to test anyone."

"Bethany?" I asked, remembering. "I think Lita's sad that she's spending the holidays abroad."

"There's a bit more to it than that. Lita probably didn't tell you this, but Bethany was occasionally quite a problematic kid."

"In what way?"

He sighed. "She was a lovely child, you know – bright, lively, full of fun. But she was volatile from the beginning, perhaps as a result of losing her father. I think Lita indulged her, too, and Bethany got used to having her own way all the time. If she was denied or refused, she'd have sudden, violent tempers. There was a bit more to it than just normal brattiness. There was never any real balance. She was as happy as could be one moment, and miserable the next. Up or down.

"It got worse as she got older. She ran away from home a few times, skipped school, fell in with the wrong crowd. There was a bit of shoplifting, which I think was probably a cry for attention. Lita finally tried to rein her in a bit, but Bethany resented her for it. It took a long, long time for them to get back on an even keel, and I'm not sure that they've managed it even now."

I felt sick for Lita. She had told me none of this, though of course there was no reason why she should have. It was a private, painful matter, not something to be shared with casual acquaintances.

"It did get better over time," Jake continued. "Bethany settled down a bit, started to behave a bit better. She caught up at school and then, finally, got into university. That was a triumphant moment for Lita, and yet it's also isolated her more than ever. Think of how it will be for her this Christmas, being all alone out there."

"Poor Lita," I said. It was such a pathetically small thing to say, but I couldn't think of anything else.

"She's done the best she could," he said, and his voice was quiet. "Ultimately, that's all anyone can do. I think we both know that."

There was a long moment of silence. The hum of voices from the village hall seemed to have quietened down a little, along with the music from the pub. I was acutely aware of

Jake's presence beside me: his tall, strong body, his quiet authority, his underlying gentleness, and his buried sorrow. I wanted to touch him. My sudden yearning was dizzying, drunken.

He said nothing, but put his hand on my arm. It was a tiny touch, and could have been interpreted as a gesture of friendliness and goodwill. Then I looked at him and saw my own longing reflected in his face. He leaned towards me, and the next thing I knew we were kissing each other.

His mouth tasted smoky, and the stubble on his jaw grazed my skin. His kiss was gentle, but sensual – so sensual that, as I stood there holding him in the cold night, I wanted nothing more than this. I wanted to be near him, with him, forever. I wanted nothing to come between us, and I wanted to forget everything that wasn't him.

Then I remembered that nothing could happen between us. Jake would stay here in Wintergreen, and I would go back to London. Before the New Year began, I'd have left this village and returned to my normal life, and we'd probably forget all about each other. And, I reflected, that was probably for the best: we wanted different lives, and we were both carrying a lot of baggage with us.

I moved away from him. For a moment we simply stood gazing at each other, both of us looking slightly dazed. Neither of us had planned or expected this, and I knew that his feelings were every bit as conflicted as mine.

"I haven't done that for ages," he said, his voice slightly hoarse.

"I know the feeling. I haven't wanted to, not for a long time."

"I know that you're divorced," he continued. "I don't pry into people's lives, but nobody can keep secrets for very long in a little place like this. I expect you've heard about my wife and daughter, too."

"Yes. I'm so sorry."

He leaned his back against the wall and looked out into the night. His eyes suddenly seemed distant, as if he could see the past playing out before him. When he spoke, his voice was little more than a murmur.

"They were the reason I came back to Wintergreen, you know. In career terms, there's no doubt that I was better off elsewhere, but when I married Patricia and we found out that there was a baby on the way it just seemed to make sense to come back here. It's a good place to raise a family: a quiet, safe area, a more relaxed pace of life. I didn't want to be one of those people who work so hard that they never see their own kids. I managed to get a transfer to Alverston, and for a few years we really were happy." He paused. "I suppose you've heard what happened next."

"Yes."

"I didn't want to live after they were gone. I wondered why I was alive when they were dead, what gave me the right – survivor's guilt, I suppose. I certainly didn't think I could carry on living in Wintergreen, when it was so full of memories. Everywhere I looked, I saw something that reminded me of them. But then, over time, that actually became something of a blessing. It was as if they lived on here, almost, as if part of them had survived and could never be taken away from me again. I suppose that sounds strange."

"No, not at all."

"I suppose what I'm trying to say is that, whatever else happens, I want to stay in Wintergreen. It's my home, and the things I love most are here. I've known nearly all these people all my life, and they got me through when I didn't think I could carry on." He paused. "I didn't intend to kiss you, Cat. I was attracted to you from the day we found Montbray's body and I saw you standing in that car park, looking and listening, not missing a thing. But I didn't think—" His voice trailed off.

"Do you think you could be with somebody else?" I asked.

"Maybe. I think Patricia would have wanted that. If she could talk to me now, I think she'd tell me to get on with my life and try to be happy. So it could happen – but, if it does, I want it to happen here, in Wintergreen." He turned and looked at me. "And that's the problem, isn't it? Because whatever you want out of your life, I'm pretty sure it isn't this."

I didn't reply for a moment. I thought of Wintergreen, of its hushed beauty. Could I be happy here? I'd have Jake, my family would be nearby, and perhaps I wouldn't have to work so hard . . . But I was addicted to my life back in London, however stressful and difficult it sometimes was. I was building my own life there, which meant a lot. You don't appreciate how much the ability to control your actions and existence means until you've lost it. When I was married, I'd given up precious freedoms and choices one by one, and then found that I'd lost them without gaining much in return. I didn't intend to make that mistake again.

"I don't think I could live here," I said. "And, even if I could, I'm nervous about getting involved with someone again. I certainly wouldn't move halfway across the country to be with somebody I didn't even know that well." I shook my head. "I need time, Jake. And time is the one thing we just don't have."

"I'm sorry." He touched my cheek, very gently, and I closed my eyes.

"So am I. But it's for the best." I opened my eyes again, and looked at him. "I hope we can be friends, though."

"Of course." He smiled, and let his hand fall. "I'll miss you when you go, Cat. But remember that, while you're still here, you can rely on me. If you need me, just call me."

"I will."

"Make sure you do. I'm a little worried about you."

"Why?"

"It's just a feeling." He shook his head. "I've got no real evidence to back it up, but I think that something's happening out on Willowgate Farm. I don't know whether it's connected to Montbray's death or not. But either way, I don't want you to get caught up in it."

I thought of the farm, of Stable Cottage, and all the things I'd experienced there. Something certainly was happening – something out of the ordinary, which I couldn't really understand. I didn't know what it was yet, but I had a feeling that I'd find out. And then I wondered exactly what I'd discover, and shivered. Some mysteries, perhaps, were best left untouched.

CHAPTER EIGHT

THERE WERE NO more strange incidents in the days that followed, though, either natural or supernatural. I slept soundly at Stable Cottage, and if there were any disturbances in the night I didn't hear them or see any evidence of them the next morning. I spent most of my time during the day at my mother's house, where I played with my nephews, helped with the last-minute preparations for Christmas, and tried to enjoy myself as much as I could. I think my mother knew that something was on my mind, and perhaps even guessed what it was, but she didn't say anything. She'd known me for long enough to know that, when I was ready to talk about something, I would.

The day before Christmas Eve, a Sunday, I got back to Stable Cottage quite late in the evening. I'd just gone inside and turned on the light when an alert sounded on my mobile phone, reminding me that it was time to pay the rent. When I'd arrived in Wintergreen, I'd arranged with Lita that I'd pay by cash or cheque at the end of every week. She usually called at the cottage on Sundays to pick the money up, but I'd spent most of the day in the village and had forgotten to leave the money on the table, where she'd find it. I counted out the money and went out again, meaning to call at the farmhouse.

Outside, the night was raw. A frigid wind swept in from the north, driving clouds before it, and as I crossed the farmyard I wondered if it would snow. I didn't think I'd ever experienced a White Christmas before, let alone one in a place as beautiful as Wintergreen, but getting around would be much more difficult in the snow. It was just as well that my mother had prepared for

Christmas so well; she had enough food, I thought, to last us all for a month.

There was no reply when I rang the doorbell, but as I stood outside I heard the sound of piano music coming from within. Lita was at home, then, which meant that the door might be unlocked. I tried the handle, and the door creaked open. For a moment I hesitated on the doorstep, feeling reluctant to enter the house without permission. I had never set foot in there before. Lita and I had always met in Stable Cottage or in the farmyard, never inside her house. She had never even invited me in for tea. I imagined that this was due to a desire for privacy on her part; but she wouldn't mind, surely, if I just handed over the rent money and then left.

Inside, the hallway was decorated with tinsel and holly, and a glittering Christmas tree had been set up, as if Lita were bravely trying to make the most of things. The door at the end of the passageway stood ajar, allowing some warm light to spill out, and it was from the room beyond that the music came. I stopped for a moment, and listened. The tune was light, unfamiliar. The occasional mistiming and mistaken note told me that it was not recorded, but that somebody was actually playing a piano in there – playing well, but not flawlessly.

"Lita?" I called softly, not wanting to alarm her. "It's Cat."

The music faltered and stopped and, though nobody replied, I heard a faint rustling sound, as of somebody moving.

"I just came by to hand over the rent money," I called again, and took a few more steps, until I stood on the threshold of the room. Peering inside, I could see that it was a comfortable living room. A fire burned in the hearth, and there was a sofa and some armchairs. I took another step, and my eyes were drawn toward the piano at the far end of the room.

The person sitting there was not Lita.

I stared at her for a long moment, puzzled, while she gazed back at me. To my surprise, she didn't seem even remotely troubled by my sudden appearance, and in fact gave me a rather impish smile. She was a young girl, not quite out of her teens: a slender girl with a vivacious, mischievous face and blond hair. She wasn't pretty, exactly, but she seemed to be full of life. She looked vaguely familiar, and I tried to remember where I had seen her before. Then I recalled the photograph that Lita had shown me, and realised that this was her daughter, Bethany.

"Hello," I said. "I'm Catrin. I'm renting Stable Cottage at the moment."

"I know," she said, surprisingly. How could she have known that, when we'd never even met?

"Is Lita at home?" I asked. "I just came over to give her the rent money."

"No. She's away at the moment." She kicked her legs back and forth in a surprisingly childlike way. "I'm Bethany, her daughter."

"I hope I didn't frighten you."

"No. I've seen you around here before."

"When? I thought you were spending the holidays abroad."

She laughed. "Is that what my mother told you?"

Something about this exchange made me feel nervous. I reached into my pocket and took out the rent money. "Can I leave the money here?" I asked.

"Yes. Just leave it on the table there, if you like."

I put the banknotes down on the coffee table she'd indicated, meaning to leave at once; but just as I was about to turn away, my curiosity got the better of me.

"You play well," I said, nodding at the piano.

"Mum used to pay for private lessons when I was younger. I had lots of different private tutors when I was a kid. Mum wanted me to go to university, make the most of my life."

"I'm sure she's very proud of you," I said.

Bethany laughed, a little bitterly.

"Do you really think so?" she asked. "I'm not so sure. She might have been, perhaps, if I'd done things her way. Unfortunately, though, I had some ideas of my own."

She tugged on the thick sweater she was wearing, as if trying to pull it further down, and as she did so I noticed a small bump there. My heart gave a little skip. It was the kind of slight bulge that I would normally put down to excess weight; but the girl sitting before me was skinny, looking as if she didn't have an ounce of spare fat on her body.

Bethany stared at me, her face utterly free of any expression.

"I'd better be going," I said uncomfortably. "I shouldn't have walked in tonight, Bethany, and I'm sorry I did. Goodnight."

I turned and walked out of the room, wanting suddenly to forget all about Lita's strange family. Bethany did not say another word or try to stop me. When I stepped out into the farmyard again and shut the door, I found that I was trembling. I walked back to Stable Cottage in a daze. What on earth was going on here?

When I got inside, I sat down and thought for a while, trying to make sense of it all. Was Bethany really pregnant? She certainly looked as if she was, but perhaps there was some other physical condition that might account for her swollen belly. Weight gain was the most obvious candidate, but Bethany did not otherwise look even slightly overweight. The main question, perhaps, was why Bethany was here at all, when Lita had said that she would be abroad throughout the holidays. Had she come back unexpectedly? Or – a curious thought – had she been here all the time, in the farmhouse, keeping out of sight? I remembered the times I had seen or sensed the presence of someone else: the sound of someone moving around in the back garden, the person who'd hidden from me in the barn. Had that person been Bethany?

I shook my head. If Bethany was pregnant, why were they so keen to keep it a secret? The circumstances might not have been ideal, but many young and unmarried women gave birth these days, and it was hardly the social disgrace it had once been. I would have thought that Lita, who had been through so much in her life, would simply have accepted it and tried to make the best of it.

Eventually, feeling at a loss, I called Jake.

"What's up?" he asked when he picked up the phone.

"I'm not quite sure," I said, and hesitated, wondering whether to say anything at all.

"Well?" He sounded mystified. "Are you going to tell me about it?"

"Only if you promise not to tell anyone else." I sighed. "I don't know exactly what's going on here, Jake, but I think I might have stumbled across a secret."

WHEN I FINISHED speaking, Jake was silent for a moment.

"None of this makes sense," he said at last. "If Bethany were pregnant, why would they want to keep it a secret? Even in a small village like this, it's hardly unheard-of, and it's not such a big thing these days. I don't think she'd have to be too worried about what people would think, or how they'd react."

"I don't know, Jake. She told me that Bethany was in France these holidays."

"That's what she told everyone. I suppose Bethany could have just changed her mind and decided that she wanted to spend Christmas at home after all."

"Maybe. I don't know, though . . . I've often felt that there was someone else here on this farm. What if it was her all along?"

"It really doesn't add up, though. Why would she feel the need to hide? Why would Lita want to hide her? And this idea of a pregnancy – I'm not sure. There could be some other reason for her appearance. You shouldn't jump to conclusions, you know. I wonder—" His voice trailed off.

"What?"

"Look," he said, "I'm going to search around a bit, see what I can find out about Bethany. I think there's something going on here, but I really don't know what it is. Don't go up to the farmhouse again tonight, Cat. Stay in the cottage, and keep the door locked."

I laughed. "I don't think I have to be afraid of Bethany, Jake. She seems pretty harmless."

"I'm sure she is, but she's not the only person out there. Look, I don't think you're likely to be in any danger, but it won't hurt to take some precautions."

"Okay," I said, though I thought he was making too much of the whole thing.

"Look after yourself, Cat. I'll come around and see you tomorrow, if that's okay."

We said goodnight, and I put down the phone. But I couldn't calm the small, nagging fear in the pit of my stomach. It was not fear of Bethany; she seemed entirely inoffensive. I had the feeling, though, that whatever was happening here had gathered momentum, and that it wouldn't be long before there was some sort of collision.

CHAPTER NINE

SHOUTING, THE SOUND of smashing glass . . . I awoke in the early hours of the next morning, turned over in my bed, and lay looking up at the ceiling. The noise had disturbed me, but it had not been part of my dreams. I lay still, and listened.

After a second or two, I heard a high, young voice – Bethany's voice. She was screaming something, and though I couldn't hear her words I recognised the venom in them. Lita's voice, when she replied, was shrill and frantic, the voice of a woman who was trying to hold things together and not altogether succeeding. I got out of bed, went to the window in the living room, and looked across at the farmhouse. A light came on in a downstairs room, and for a brief moment I caught sight of Lita's white, haunted face. Then she pulled the curtain across, and the farmyard was plunged into darkness.

All went quiet for a while, but I could not sleep again. I got up and made some tea, tried to read and found that I couldn't concentrate, and then put on the radio and sat on the sofa, thinking. I turned the volume right down, not wanting to disturb either Bethany or Lita or attract their attention. I felt that their argument probably had something to do with my having met Bethany the previous evening, and wished that I had never gone to the farmhouse. Perhaps Lita was offended or embarrassed, and would ask me to leave in the morning. I could hardly blame her. Perhaps, on the other hand, it would all turn out to have been a huge misunderstanding, which I hoped – but did not believe – would be the case.

A miserable hour passed, during which I sat still and wondered and worried. Then another sound cut through the hush of night.

I heard the farmhouse door creaking open, followed by footsteps and a dragging sound. I turned off the light, went to the window and moved the curtain aside. The light above the farmhouse door had been turned on, and I could see Lita, wearing a heavy coat, hauling a large suitcase towards her car. Bethany followed close behind, with a sports bag slung across her shoulder. Her small face was sullen and tear-stained, her body hidden beneath a large puffer jacket.

Lita opened the car boot and lifted the suitcase inside, and then took the sports bag from Bethany, who said something in a petulant tone. Lita put her hand to her head, as if she was suffering from a headache, and looked momentarily crushed. Then she seemed to rally, said something in a low voice, and stroked Bethany's cheek.

Bethany got into the passenger seat of the car, and Lita went to turn off the light – but, though she had shut the farmhouse door, I saw that she hadn't locked it. Probably she was too miserable and distracted to remember. Then she got into the driver's seat, and the engine throbbed in the quiet night. The headlights threw a ghostly light over the farmyard, and wheels crunched on the cobbles as she drove slowly away. I stood watching as the headlights picked out naked branches, and then faded into the night as the car turned the corner.

What was going on now? Leaving home before dawn on Christmas Eve, taking luggage with them . . . surely an argument, however heated, wouldn't lead them to do that. Lita might be feeling embarrassed, hurt and angry even, but running away like this wouldn't change much. If Bethany was indeed pregnant, their reactions seemed out of all proportion. Who was the father, I wondered, and what exactly had happened?

A horrible suspicion glimmered in my mind – unlikely on the surface, but with an underlying plausibility.

I looked across at the quiet, dark farmhouse, remembering that Lita had not locked the door before she left. Since she had taken a suitcase with her, it was likely that they were going quite some distance, and wouldn't be back for a while. I stood still for a moment, thinking.

I hadn't forged a career in journalism by having a scrupulous regard for people's privacy. Distasteful as that was, it was undeniably true. Journalists pried, questioned, probed; sometimes people were hurt or embarrassed as a result. I wasn't proud of that, but I'd come to regard it as an inevitable part of the job. And besides, I thought, anything would be better than cowering behind locked doors all night.

I threw on some jeans and a sweater, and prepared to go outside.

THE TEMPERATURE HAD dropped and, as I walked across the farmyard, a few snowflakes drifted down from the sky. I heard a cow lowing and the wind whining in Foxhay Brake, and shivered. The farmhouse stood stark and black against the night sky: a place of silence, and of secrets.

The farmhouse door was unlocked, just as I'd thought. It opened with a creak that made me wince, even though I knew that nobody was at home. I stepped inside, and turned on the hallway light. The house was eerily silent, and somehow the Christmas decorations just added to the gloom of the atmosphere.

I made my way first to the living room, where I had met Bethany the previous evening. My rent money lay on the coffee table, apparently untouched, next to a half-empty cup of tea. Glancing into the corner, I saw the shattered remains of a drinking glass. I supposed that either Lita or Bethany had smashed it during their argument. Elsewhere, though, the house seemed to be entirely normal. The kitchen was neat and tidy, with dishes left to dry beside the sink and a loaf of bread on the work surface. I went into a small office room, where I imagined Lita dealt with business and paperwork. A computer and printer stood on top of a tidy desk, and various papers had been put into a meticulously neat pile. I glanced through them, and found them to be bills, invoices, receipts, and official communications of various kinds. Nothing out of the ordinary.

I crept up the stairs, and looked into the bathroom first. There was a small puddle on the floor next to the shower cubicle, as if someone had used it just a short time before. A cabinet was stuffed with cosmetics and make-up, along with some standard over-the-counter medicines like aspirin and painkillers. If Bethany was pregnant, she must need medical attention; but how did she ever manage to see doctors, if she was kept in the house all the time? There was nothing in the cabinet, at any rate, to shed any light on the matter.

I went into the bedrooms. There was a neat, barely-touched room at the end of the corridor that I took to be a guest bedroom. Next to it was a larger room that I supposed must be Bethany's. It was a pretty room, well cared-for, in which the overwhelming colour was a very soft light green. A rug with a floral design was spread over the polished wooden floorboards, and the furniture was simple, modern, probably Scandinavian. There were a few books, mostly popular novels, interspersed with some classics and a handful of school or university textbooks. A small flat-screen TV was fixed to the wall opposite a neat single bed. Despite the room's tidiness, it had a lived-in feel; the quilt on the bed was slightly rumpled, and a scrunched-up tissue had been left on the bedside table. Simple, casual clothes, typical teenagers' clothes such as jeans and sweatshirts, hung in the wardrobe. Yet there were also several empty hangers, suggesting that some items of clothing had been removed.

It was an innocent room, I thought, a room that might belong to any indulged middle-class teenage girl. There was no sign here of the storms that had hit Bethany's mind, nothing to indicate that she was expecting a baby. Perhaps she'd become as skilled as her mother at hiding these things.

Feeling guilty, I opened the drawer in the bedside table a fraction, and then paused as I caught sight of a blurry, indistinct, black-and-white image lying within. I took it out and looked at it more closely. For a moment I could not be sure what it was, but then I made out the shape of a tiny head and body. It was an ultrasound image of an unborn baby.

I stood still for a moment or two, feeling my heart jump. It was true, then: Bethany was expecting a baby. It occurred to me that, in all likelihood, Lita's stories about her spending her holidays in France were just useful lies, designed to throw people off the scent. And perhaps Bethany had been here at Willowgate Farm all the time, keeping out of sight, but occasionally wandering outside after dark, and almost being seen on a few occasions . . .

I put the image back into the drawer, closed it, and then left the room.

I went to Lita's bedroom last, feeling a pang of guilt at intruding upon the privacy of the woman who had treated me with such kindness. At first glance, it was just another ordinary room. A large double bed with a beige quilt and a mound of matching pillows and cushions stood against one wall. Some clothes – a skirt and a red blouse – had been neatly folded and placed on a chair, and a pair of high-heeled shoes was on the floor, one of them lying on its side. Cosmetics and make-up had been piled upon a dressing-table, along with hair clips and some obviously expensive jewellery.

A folded newspaper had been left on the bedside table. I picked it up, and found that it was the local paper, and had been left open at the Lost and Found column. I scanned the print, and found the short, terse item about the lost watch. My heart jumped a little. Coincidence, or something else?

I put the paper back down, trying to leave it in the same position as before, and went over to the wardrobe. Lita's clothes were neatly divided into the smart outfits she wore for business meetings and the more casual clothes she used around the farm. The wardrobe was filled almost to capacity, which suggested that Lita had not taken any clothes with her and was not planning to stay away for very long. The thought served as an unpleasant reminder that I'd better hurry up and leave as quickly as I could.

I was just about the close the wardrobe door when I noticed something hanging in the corner. It was a large black coat, made of either fur or imitation fur. I ran my hands over its sleeve, and remembered what Jake had told me about the fibres that had been found on Montbray's body: a mixture of acrylic and modacrylic polymers, often associated with the manufacture of imitation fur.

"My God," I whispered; and in that moment I heard the sound of a car approaching the farmhouse.

I DIDN'T DARE hope that it would be anyone other than Lita. Who else, after all, could possibly be driving up to the farmhouse in the early hours of the morning, when it was still dark outside? The farm workers arrived later. My heart seemed to hang suspended in my chest for a moment, and then I heard the sounds of a brake being applied and the engine being killed. It spurred me to action, and I quickly reviewed my options. I had no chance of getting out of the house without being seen. I could simply walk downstairs and try to brazen it out, try to think of some innocent reason why I was in the house at such a time – but of course, there *was* no such reason, and nothing I could say would convince Lita otherwise. Whatever else she was, she wasn't stupid.

And – the thought struck me like a blow – if she really had killed Hugo Montbray, she would be a desperate woman, and willing to go to extreme lengths to protect herself and her daughter.

I snapped off the bedroom light and crept over to the guest bedroom I had seen earlier. The downstairs light was still on, I saw, and I had no time to go down and turn it off. I could only hope that Lita would think that she had left it on herself. I wondered if I'd left any other evidence of my having been here. It was too late to worry about it now; I'd just have to hope for the best.

I shut the bedroom door behind me just as the front door opened downstairs. I heard

Lita enter the house, heard her footsteps falter as she found the light on. A long moment passed, during which the world seemed to hold its breath, and then I heard the front door click quietly shut again. There was another hesitant footstep down in the hallway, and my heart sank. Clearly Lita had guessed that something was wrong, and was thinking things over, working out what to do next.

I positioned myself behind the bedroom door, hoping that, if Lita did come in, she'd simply take a cursory look around before going out again. I shrank back against the wall, barely daring to breathe, frightened that the slightest movement or noise would give me away.

Slow, light footsteps sounded on the stairs – the sound of someone moving carefully, listening, weighing each sight and sound. She paused at the top of the stairs, and then took a tentative step in the direction of the guest bedroom. My heart gave a painful thud. Then she paused again, and turned away. I heard her go into the bathroom, and then the sound of running water and cabinet doors being opened and closed. She stayed there for about five minutes, and then came out and made her way to her own room. I heard her footsteps tapping lightly, followed by the click of the bedroom door.

Everything went quiet. I breathed out and opened my eyes, which I had kept closed before. Had she decided that there was nothing to worry about after all, and gone to bed? It seemed too much to hope for, but it wasn't impossible. I looked around, wondering what to do next. I glanced out of the window and saw snowflakes falling like flowers from the sky, coming thick and fast now, and no doubt settling on the ground. It looked like it would snow for a long time to come, for hours. I had to get out of here.

I took my phone out of my pocket. The screen lit up, casting an eerie glow over the room, and I tapped out a message to Jake.

"I'm in the farmhouse," I typed. "Lita drove Bethany away somewhere this morning, and then came back while I was looking around. I'm trapped in an upstairs room. I think she might have killed Montbray. Please come as soon as you can."

I sent the message on its way with a silent prayer, and put the phone back in my pocket.

Time seemed to slow down to a crawl. I didn't dare to sneak out of the house just yet, and there was nothing else I could do in the meantime. I sat down on the side of the bed, wincing as the mattress creaked beneath my weight, and listened for any sound or movement from within the house. Everything seemed quiet – suspiciously so, I thought. And yet as the minutes passed I allowed myself to hope. Perhaps Lita had been so tired that she had gone straight to bed, either not registering the signs that someone had been in the house or disregarding them. Perhaps she was now sleeping quietly, the deep and deadened sleep that sometimes comes in the wake of exhaustion and grief. But the thought of taking my chances and trying to leave seemed impossible, terrifying.

Had she really killed Hugo Montbray? What had her reason been? I remembered the ultrasound image in Bethany's bedside table, and the fact that Montbray was said to have been a womaniser. But Lita had wept for Montbray after his death, had suggested to me that she was his friend as well as his business partner. Was she capable of murder? I didn't have much evidence, I reminded myself: a copy of a local newspaper, and a coat of the kind that probably hung in thousands of wardrobes throughout the country. Even to my suspicious mind, it wasn't very compelling.

Eventually the first smudge of dawn appeared in the sky outside: a slight dilution of the darkness, a hint of grey and then pink in the east. I crept over to the window and looked outside. A thick carpet of white lay on the ground, and the snow was still falling. It was Christmas Eve. Did the farm workers arrive as normal on Christmas Eve? I supposed they would have to; the animals would need to be looked after as usual, whatever the date. In any case, the working day started early on farms. It wouldn't be long before Lita was up and about.

.

It was now or never. I couldn't afford to dither any longer; I had to get out of the house, and I had to do it now.

I went to the bedroom door, listened, heard nothing. I opened it a crack and peered out into the corridor. It was still dark, but the windows admitted just enough light for me to make out the bedroom doors and the stairs. Lita's bedroom was on the opposite side of the house, and the door was firmly closed. If I moved quietly, there was a good chance she wouldn't hear me.

I tiptoed over to the stairs, flinching as a floorboard creaked. I stopped for a moment, and listened. Nothing. At the top of the stairs, I looked down, paused, and put my hand on the banister. The farmhouse was old, and the steps were worn and irregular. I'd have to tread slowly and with care. I put out one foot, felt around with it, and found the step below. It gave a very slight squeak as I stepped down onto it. I hesitated, and in that moment my heart jumped as I heard a faint noise, as of somebody moving nearby. But I couldn't stop now; I had no choice but to carry on.

I had just put my foot down on the next step when the lights suddenly snapped on, dazzling me. I turned and looked up. Lita stood at the top of the stairs, fully dressed, with a look of cold fury in her eyes that I had never seen before.

"GOING SOMEWHERE, CAT?" she asked. Her voice was icy and full of hate. She took a step towards me, and I glanced over my shoulder. The steps lay beneath me, steep and uneven. It would be a long way to fall.

There was nothing for it but to tell the truth, I realised. If she were innocent, she'd soon set me straight; perhaps she'd even laugh about it. I looked back up at her.

"I'm sorry," I said. "I heard you and Bethany arguing last night, and saw you leave in the car. I thought—"

"You thought you'd come over here and snoop around a bit. I might have guessed. What exactly were you looking for?"

"I was curious. You see, I met Bethany last night, quite by accident. I came to the farmhouse to give you the rent money—"

"And you realised that she was expecting."

"It was just a guess." I decided to try to engage Lita in conversation – the more she talked, the less time she would have to do anything else. "Why didn't you want anyone to know, Lita? It's not such a big thing these days."

"I think you can probably guess why, Cat." To my surprise, tears prickled in her eyes. "It's not really the fact that she's pregnant that bothers me; it's the identity of the father."

"Hugo Montbray," I said. Of course: everyone had said that he was a womaniser and had broken a string of hearts. It wasn't so surprising that he might have fathered a child or two. But Bethany – she was years younger than him, and vulnerable. When Lita had found out, she must have been furious – furious enough to kill, perhaps.

"Bethany had turned her life around," Lita said, and a tear leaked out of her eye and trickled down her cheek. "Things were changing. She'd gone to university, made new friends; she seemed to be enjoying herself, making a new life. But something was different. I didn't realise what it was, not for a long time. I should have known, should have seen . . . Bethany is trusting. Say what you like about her, but she's always been sincere, and she thinks that everyone else is the same. She listens to people's lies and doesn't even realise that they *are* lies. She never even suspects. And she gives her heart, in a matter of moments, and never thinks of the consequences." Lita clenched and unclenched her fists, and her tears ran faster. "I'd always known that Hugo was a womaniser, but I never thought he'd target Bethany. He'd known her since she was a little girl, and I was his business partner – his friend, or so I thought. I defended him while everyone else was damning him. I stood by him . . . I think it began during the summer, before she even left for university. He was spending a lot of time at the farm, overseeing the work on Stable Cottage, and he noticed her – noticed her in a new way, I suppose. She wasn't a girl anymore. He moved in on her, paid her compliments, bought her presents. He made her feel special, I suppose. And she was too young and too innocent to know better."

She set her foot down on the top step. Her face was a crazed mask of grief. I moved down onto a lower step.

"At some point," she continued, "an affair began. I don't know when, exactly. They had plenty of opportunity, because I was so busy with work and different things. I saw the change in her, of course, but I thought it was because she was getting older, becoming a woman. I never guessed, never imagined – what a fool I was! And all the time Hugo was taking advantage of her, promising her the earth. He didn't mean a word of it, of course, but she listened to him. She went to university at the end of the summer because she thought he'd be waiting for her, working hard so that one day they could have a whole new life together.

"About halfway through the term she came back here for a few days, and that was when it all began to fall apart. He was unconcerned, not nearly as attentive and affectionate as before. Of course, he'd tired of her, had already moved on to the next woman. She knew she was expecting by then, but she kept it from me. She didn't know what to do. She tried to talk to him, but he didn't want to know."

I could see from the greyness of the light that it would soon be day. Jake would get my message, and would come as soon as he could. *Just a little bit longer*, I told myself. *Just keep her talking, make the time pass . . .*

"I only found out a few weeks ago," Lita said. "Bethany knew she couldn't hide it for much longer, so she turned up here one day and admitted everything. She couldn't face anyone else knowing about it. She felt humiliated, used. But the worst thing was that she'd never be able to get away from Hugo. He would always be there, living just a short distance from her, and still refusing to acknowledge that the child was even his. I thought that if I could only talk to him, if I could only find some way to make him understand . . ."

"You killed him, Lita."

"It wasn't intentional. Believe me, I didn't go out to Foxhay Brake that evening meaning to kill him. I arranged to meet him out there. He didn't want to see me, of course, but I made it very clear that he wasn't going to get rid of me until he agreed to talk to me – not unless he wanted a confrontation in his house, or in the middle of the street in town. I tried to be calm when we met, I tried to explain things to him. I told him the baby was his responsibility, and that he should at least accept that. I thought there might be a core of decency in the man . . . He just laughed. Said that Bethany had been a bit of fun, but that he hadn't made her any promises and didn't owe her anything. He implied that the baby might not even be his; Bethany had always been trouble, so what made me think that he was the only man she'd been with? Who'd take her word against his?

"Everything went sort of quiet and still at that point. I knew I wouldn't be able to persuade him to do the right thing, and I saw for myself what he was really like. I could say that I lost my temper, but it didn't feel like that; I felt very calm, actually. I felt that things had been set in motion and wouldn't be stopped, and that I had no choice but to play my part. I walked towards him, barely knowing what I was doing anymore, and the next thing I knew he was standing at the very edge of the gully, swaying back and forth, trying to keep his balance. He grabbed at me, trying to save himself. I gave him another push. He didn't even have time to cry out. I heard a cracking sound and a splash, and looked down over the edge of the gully. I could see him lying there, in the stream, and I knew that he was dead. I was glad. He didn't deserve to live."

"How did Bethany react when she found out?"

"She still doesn't know. I've made sure of that. She had feelings for the man, and it would kill her if she knew. I've kept her here, away from all the gossip. I want to give her time to get over him. She'll have the baby in peace, and that will help her to forget, and when I tell her that he's gone – well, perhaps it won't be so bad. That's what I planned, at least. But then *you* turned up, Cat."

"I didn't mean to interfere, Lita."

"Perhaps you didn't at first. You came so close to finding out anyway. Bethany was always interested in people, and she'd sneak out of the house sometimes, spy on you. Remember that night when you thought there were burglars in the barn? It was her. That wasn't your fault, of course. But this – coming into our house, intruding like this—"

"I'm sorry."

"It doesn't matter whether you're sorry or not. You've done it, and it can't be undone."

She took another step, and I began to back away, moving slowly, feeling for the step below. Lita had been driven mad, I thought – by sorrow, perhaps – and her moral compass had been shattered. She had killed once, and she'd kill again if she had to.

"I won't tell anyone else, Lita."

"Won't you?" She gave me a cold smile. "I can't believe that. You're a journalist, aren't you? Have you been writing a story about this? How's the story going to end, do you think?"

"I'm not writing a story."

"Perhaps not. But you seem to have become very close to a certain policeman. Do you mean to tell me that you're not going to share all of this with him? I can't believe that."

"Lita—"

What happened next seemed to occur in slow motion, one frame at a time. Lita moved towards me, arms outstretched. I felt the impact as something hit my body, pushing me backwards. I let go of the banister, out of sheer surprise I think, and teetered for a moment on the edge of the step, trying to regain my balance. Hopeless . . . the world turned a somersault over my head as I fell. For a strange, timeless moment I seemed to hang suspended in space – and then I felt an intense jolt that seemed to run through my entire body, and heard a sickening crack.

I was lying at the bottom of the staircase. For a moment I thought nothing, felt nothing . . . and then a hammer blow of pain shot through my left arm, and I gasped. Yet I realised that I'd been lucky, too. My arm had taken the main impact of my fall, and though it was injured – broken, perhaps – the rest of my body seemed relatively unharmed. I struggled to sit up; and as I did so I became aware of the distant sound of a car engine, approaching slowly and painfully through the snow. Grey daylight trickled through the window. *Please let it be Jake*, I thought. *Please, Jake, hurry.*

I don't know if Lita even heard the car. She seemed to pause for a moment and listen, her head turned slightly to one side. But even if she was aware of it, she didn't stop – and there was a sense, I supposed, in which she couldn't stop. The wheel had been set in motion, and had gained a momentum of its own, and she couldn't bring it to a standstill, not even if she wanted to. She'd killed Montbray and now, if she wanted to save herself from the consequences, she'd have to kill me.

She began to descend the stairs, taking her time, moving in a slow motion that seemed almost hypnotic. Was there still a glimmer of conscience in her, a reluctance to kill? I like to think so. I like to think that she was stalling, that some part of her didn't want to do this after all.

The car engine stopped just short of the farmhouse, and I heard a car door open and close. Boots crunched on fresh snow.

"Jake!" I screamed; and a moment later I heard someone pounding on the front door, shaking the handle. I realised with a sinking heart that Lita had locked it from the inside, but Jake didn't stop. I watched as the door shook in its frame; and then something crashed against it with such force that the entire house seemed to tremble, and it gave slightly. There was a pause, and another crash. The door burst open, and Jake half-fell into the hallway, surrounded by a flurry of snow.

I looked up at Lita, who was halfway down the stairs. She stood still and looked down at him, and now she looked calm and utterly tearless. She knew it was all over, and I think she was almost relieved that it was. It had all been taken out of her hands at last –

the trouble, the responsibility, the anguish –
and I felt that it came as a release. For a
moment, she almost smiled; and then she
took another step, and held out her hands,
almost as if she was inviting him to cuff them.

Then all the light in the world was
eclipsed, darkness fell around me, and I knew
no more.

CHAPTER TEN

THERE'S THIS TO be said for a close brush with death: it gives you a new perspective on life. For the first time in years, I found that I was content to simply sit and take things as they were. With a broken arm, sprained ankle and several cuts and bruises, I suppose there was very little else I could actually do. I couldn't even type, unless I did so with one hand, which proved to be time-consuming and frustrating. So my laptop remained unopened and my work went neglected, and I found that I really didn't miss it that much.

I spent much of Christmas Eve in hospital in Alverston, but I made it back to Wintergreen for Christmas Day, armed with some painkillers. I spent much of that day lazing around and trying to persuade everyone that I was fine, which felt like a lie. Physically I'd heal, but I wondered if any other scars would linger once these holidays had finished. Eventually I decided that there was very little point in worrying about it. From now on, I vowed, I'd take things as they came and not give too much thought to tomorrow.

By the time evening came the excitement of the day was largely spent. My nephews were in bed, and Adam and Sandy had gone to visit some friends in the village. My mother and stepfather were in the kitchen, clearing up after a long and rather trying day, during which they'd valiantly tried to celebrate Christmas as normal. When I looked at my mother, though, I knew that my ordeal had, in a sense, been harder for her than for me.

"Cat," she'd asked, "what were you *thinking* of?"

Jake had asked me something similar. And the worst thing was that I didn't really have any good answers.

Lita had been arrested, of course. She had confessed, and in many ways seemed glad that it was all over. In spite of everything, I found myself feeling sorry for her. Her life had been marked by one tragedy after another, starting with the death of her husband. She'd done all she could to make her daughter happy, and in the end she'd been defeated even in that simple, honourable quest. I hoped that the justice system would go easy on her, and I hoped too that no further harm would come to Bethany.

I sat back and tried not to think about it. It was out of my hands now, anyway; all I could do was let the police deal with things, and hope for the best.

The doorbell rang, and I heard my stepfather padding out into the hall to answer it. Then I heard the low murmur of Jake's voice, and a moment later he came into the living room. He'd taken off his coat and boots, and his face was red with cold. He smiled, but I could see from the shadows under his eyes that he'd found the last couple of days almost as trying as I had.

"I wanted to make sure you were all right," he said, sitting down next to me. "I didn't have the chance to say much to you yesterday."

"I'm fine."

"Good." He shook his head. "Frankly, you can thank your lucky stars that you got out of it with just a broken arm. Of all the stupid things to do . . . If this is how you carry on in London, I'm amazed you haven't got yourself killed by now."

"Funnily enough, London's beginning to seem like a pretty safe place, compared to Wintergreen." I sighed. "How's Bethany?"

"Hard to say. She's being looked after by relatives over in Alverston, I understand, but I don't think she's been told about her mother's arrest yet. God only knows how she'll react when she hears about it."

"Poor kid. She doesn't even know that Montbray's dead yet. And from what Lita told me, she might still be hoping that things could work out between them. History repeating itself, perhaps." I remembered Patience, and the odd things I'd experienced in Stable Cottage. "There are so many parallels between what happened to Bethany and Patience. It's almost as if the Montbray curse had been set in motion again."

"The Montbrays are a pretty bedevilled lot," Jake said. "Sometimes they almost seemed to be chasing their own ruin. Maybe that's how curses are fulfilled. There's no need for magic. You just give somebody a nudge in the right direction, get them to set off on the road to self-destruction. Perhaps, on some level, the Montbrays always believed that they were cursed."

Outside, the wind picked up and ruffled the trees, sending a flurry of snow flying past the window. I thought about Stable Cottage. No one would be sleeping there tonight; it would be dark, cold and empty – or not empty, perhaps. I shivered.

"I've never been a great believer in the supernatural, you know," I said, "but I'm glad I won't be going back to Stable Cottage tonight. Perhaps something lingers there after all. A mood, a shadow – I don't know what, exactly. I felt it, though."

Jake was silent for a moment. I looked at his downcast eyes, his strong-featured face that was also sensitive, and wished things could be different. An impossible wish, of course. Time was slipping away from us, and I couldn't stop it.

"I've always felt," he said at last, "that something of us carries on, even after we've gone. Sentimental rubbish, some might say, and not something that I can offer any convincing arguments for. It's just a feeling, but I'm glad I have it. Perhaps it's something to do with living in a place like Wintergreen. You feel the weight of history round here; it's there, beside you, and no less real than the present. It's as if, on some level, things never changed at all. Does that sound stupid?"

"Not to me. I'm glad you feel that way."

He got up and went to stand by the window. Outside, the snow lay thick on the ground. The bell in the church tower began to ring, and he smiled, very faintly, as he listened to it.

"Are you sure I can't persuade you to stay, Cat?" he asked quietly, not looking at me.

I tried to imagine what it would be like if I did stay. I thought of being with him, sleeping beside him, waking up next to him. For a moment, I wanted it more than anything. But then I thought of the other things that might happen. I'd miss the excitement of London and the independence I'd found there. I'd be a long way from colleagues and professional opportunities, and far from the places where the news I reported was made. What would happen once the first flush of romance had worn off? Would we end up resenting each other? I didn't want to be haunted by yet another failure.

I got up, a little awkwardly given my sprained ankle, and went to stand next to him.

"Part of me wishes I could," I said, "but you know I can't."

"I suppose you're right." He turned to me. "Can I kiss you anyway?"

"I'll be quite upset if you don't, Jake."

His lips touched mine in the gentlest of kisses. Across the village, the church bell rang out in a joyful little tune, and another flurry of snow drifted past the window. I thought of the miles that lay between here and London, and how much I'd miss this man and this place. What would happen to me when these holidays came to an end, and what would I do next?

I put the question from my mind. This moment was mine and his, and I wouldn't let anything ruin it.

After all, I'd learned to let tomorrow take care of itself.

AUTHOR NOTE

Thank you for reading *Wintergreen*. I hope you enjoyed it. If you'd like to know more about my books, you can visit my website at maribiella.com, or catch up with me on Twitter, Facebook or Goodreads. You can sign up to my newsletter for gifts, giveaways, exclusives and updates at http://eepurl.com/bXqUnX .

Reviews help other readers to discover books. I appreciate all reviews, whether positive or negative.